COOLING CREA

Explicit & Forbidden Erotic Hot Sexy Stories for Naughty Adult Box Set

Collection

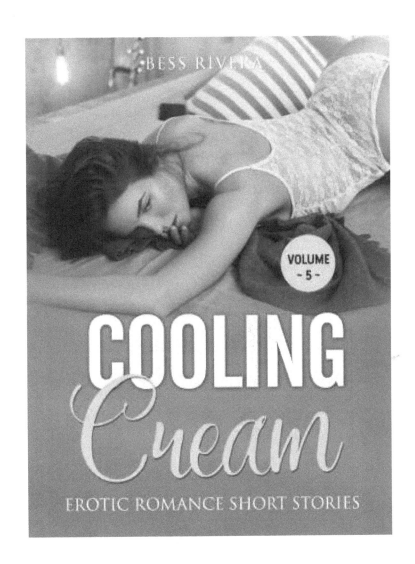

Bess Rivera

TABLE OF CONTENT

Two pairs of circular pupils peered through the inky darkness, their yellow irises searching the area for a suitable prey. The night was friendlier to these creatures because they can see six times as much as they can during the day.

A few feet away from them, the local pub was radiant with brilliant, blinking lights, the holiday season had brought joy and good cheer to the otherwise drab ambiance of the pub.

Tina Peterson was busy serving beer to the store's patrons, and taking orders for food and snacks. She was smart, attractive and witty, but most men avoided her like the plague because of her height and chubby figure. She was about 6 feet tall and weighed 260 pounds. That was why at 20, she was still a certified virgin with no chance of being asked out for a date.

The pairs of yellow eyes watched Tina closely from the shadows, their light yellow and orange stripes hidden by the thick foliage. They were 3.5 feet in height and 10.1 feet in length - lovely to look at but ferocious in nature.

For years, Tom Smith and Ted Parker had scoured the town for a suitable mate, but unluckily, they only encountered 'sickly' and emaciated females that were not worthy of raising their progeny.

The two creatures purred and rubbed their noses against each other, communicating through their eyes. Their yellow irises turned brown and then changed to a deep blue color. Their heads started becoming rounder and their furs disappeared from their bodies. "Argggh," They roared wildly, their clawed hands turning into human hands and their hind legs, into feet. After a few minutes of bone crushing conversion, their human transformation was completed. Their tiger forms had fully morphed into humans. They were were-tigers, out to find a mate who can propagate their species.

"Tom, I think we've finally found a healthy and perfect mate," the younger one aired his thoughts.

"Yes, I agree with you Ted. This is the one," Tom was confident they had finally found her.

Tom buttoned the light blue shirt on his broad chest and put on the faded jeans to complete his outfit. Ted was wearing the same outfit but with a different color – purple.

They sauntered towards the pub with a swagger. They were both over 6 feet tall, their bronzed bodies bursting with well-toned muscles. Tom was auburn haired, while Ted was dark-haired. Their blue eyes were glossy and brooding, their noses sharp, complimenting their wide luscious lips. They were strikingly handsome, and at first glance they could be mistaken as twins, who were out for a night out. All eyes turned towards them as they entered the pub.

"Yes, gentlemen, what will you have?"

"Beer, please," Tom said, eyeing Tina thoughtfully.

"Same here," Ted echoed, thinking how good she smelled. She left in the air a trace of the odor of a delectable ambar deer. Ted's mouth watered that he wanted to bite her smooth neck and devour her. His insides churned - aroused. He shook his head to erase the image.

"Oh, by the way, I'm Tom and this is Ted," Tom offered Tina a broad grin.

"Jess, here," she smiled back, and left them in a jiffy before they were able to say more.

After 15 minutes, Tina was back with their frothing, sparkling beers. "Enjoy your beers," she beamed at them.

After two more beers ordered from another waitress, the two shape shifters decided to call it a night.

"She's too busy," Ted remarked, "we'll have to come back."

They left the pub feeling frustrated and hungry. They morphed back into their tiger forms and prowled the forest hunting for food. They were hoping to encounter werewolves, but not even a whiff of the vile creatures appeared.

***

After three days, they went back to the pub. As usual, it was another busy night for Tina.

They greeted her and tried to strike a conversation. "Hi Tom and Ted, "Tina remembered them.

She was in a pink, knitted sweater that enclosed her big, front melons. Ted gulped and Tom stared. They were helplessly drawn to her, and their need for her was growing day by day.

"Can we invite you for some pizza after work?" Ted cleared his throat nervously.

"Oh," Tina was taken aback. "Ummm…I have a previous commitment," she blurted out. She was surprised because they were still strangers to her.

"I see. Well then perhaps tomorrow? Or the day after? Whatever day you're available," Ted was persistent. He was stroking his thick thighs suggestively.

Tina blushed and felt hot. Beads of sweat mushroomed in her armpits and forehead.

"I'm… not… sure," she stammered. "Okay, no pressure," Tom replied.

And, again, they left without any hint of success in sight.

"This is unacceptable," Ted roared in his animalistic voice, his irises turning yellow. "How can she refuse us?"

"Hey, she's all human. They have a peculiar way of wooing their mates," he appeased him. "Be patient. We have to devise another plan."

Ted morphed and his claws curved to grab a skittering mouse, muttering to himself in his fading consciousness, "to hell with musophobia!"

The were-tigers roamed the forest, getting rid of their angst and frustration. They were the last of their species and they wanted to propagate their lineage with a worthy human female before their demise. After 10 years of existence, they knew that their time was drawing near. If they didn't succeed in their endeavor, their species would become extinct. It was their final quest to produce an offspring.

***

The subsequent plan that they hatched was to apply as bouncers for the pub. With their bulky bodies and brawny arms, they got the job without sweat. It was a breeze getting closer to Tina afterwards.

"So, you're our bouncers now?" Tina seemed pleased, but there was still a vestige of doubt reflected in her eyes.

"Uh huh, we are," they affirmed.

They're like caged tigers, Tina thought, ready to pounce on their prey.

It was past midnight but Tina was still plying the tables. Tom and

Ted were overjoyed that Tina was still on duty. They had intended to force her to join them for some drinks after work.

When the last customer left, Ted closed the gap between him and Tina. "Jess, can you join us for some drinks."

"Here?" her eyes opened wide in astonishment. It was the first time someone invited her to join them for some drinks.

"If you like, but we can also go somewhere for a change of ambiance," Tom replied, his heart doing a double flip.

"Well…" she hesitated - reluctant - because of her inferiority complex. They were no longer strangers but she didn't believe that the two men were genuinely interested in her. She had always been the wallflower of any group.

"C'mon, we won't eat you," they joked, thinking, but we can eat you down there.

Tina scrutinized them closely and she sensed something weird about them. The color of their eyes shifted to yellow, black and brown every now and then. She shivered. Perhaps it was due to the flickering lights, she surmised.

"Umm, okay," she finally acquiesced. "But I won't be able to stay long."

They decided to try the 24/7 Flamingo club located a few blocks away.

When they arrived, only three tables were occupied and the band was playing a popular song of the 90s, Whitney Houston's 'I Will Always Love You'.

"Perfect for a slow dance," Ted mumbled to Tina. "Sorry, I don't dance."

"Don't say that. You can always learn," he pulled Tina to her feet and led her to the dance floor.

Ted's strapping arms crushed her to him; both of his hands were holding her on her waist. "Your hands should be around my neck," he taught her how.

Their abrupt body contact sent sparks through Tina's body, making her tremble. Ted had the same reaction. He felt like a bolt of lightning had coursed through his veins and into his bloodstream.

She gave in. On the floor, her steps were measured and hesitant. She almost stepped on his toes as they waltzed around the floor.

"Relax, don't struggle against me," he murmured to her ears. "Close your eyes and enjoy this moment. Take my lead." His breath, smelling of fresh grass and morning dew, was hot on her ears. If she turned a fraction of her head to the left, their lips would meet. In spite of her best efforts to remain calm, she hyperventilated.

Tina was hypnotized by Ted's eyes drilling into hers. They were changing colors again, as if in warning. But Tina didn't take heed. She was lost in the warmth of the enticing arms of Ted, floating on cloud nine, as she surrendered herself to Ted's expert maneuvers.

She was awakened from her semi-sleep when she felt a hard object pressing against the lower part of her abdomen. She looked down and gasped when she noticed that it was Ted's erection that was protruding from his jeans. Oh God! That's huge, she thought. She was thrilled that she had such power over a man – a power that she had longed for since she started imagining making love to a man. Her slit quivered, wanting to envelope the big mass of meat throbbing underneath his jeans. She was horny and her body was aflame with the fires of lust.

Ted was delirious with passion. His animal instinct told him to crush her and fuck the hell out of her, but through brute strength, he was able to hold back his carnal need. A tap on his shoulder made them turn. It was Tom asking for a dance. Ted gave in without a word.

Tom glided her expertly around the dance floor, his body swaying in unison with the music. Instead of holding her with both hands on her waist as Ted did, Tom held only one of her hands. Tina's fever didn't subside, instead it tripled and her body was now a burning flesh of passion. She wanted to be made love to – a dream she always had.

She tipped her head upwards and offered her trembling lips to Tom, running a wet tongue over her lower lip.

Tom mumbled something unintelligible and his lips came crashing down on hers, his tongue seeking hers. His fingers were now kneading one of her tits through her sweater. Such soft and big tits, he sighed, raring to fuck her.

Just then, the band shifted to a modern song, and the dim lights were changed into a kaleidoscope of brilliant colors. They dragged their bodies forcibly away from each other and trudged back to their seats, their bodies on fire.

Tina became self-conscious under the brighter lights of the bar. She had always felt inferior about her body, but the recent attention coming from Tom and Ted had started to boost her self-confidence.

"You're beautiful!" Ted reassured her, seemingly able to read her thoughts.

She looked at him incredulously, and shook her head, "You're drunk," she muttered.

"Jess, you're indeed, gorgeous!" Tom reiterated. "In fact, you're perfect. Your teeth, your smile, your hair, your body - everything is perfect."

"You don't have to butter me up, boys. You just want to get laid, right?" she asked, unabashed.

The two were-tigers exchanged glances and snarled impishly, "This woman is brave," Tom exclaimed. "Yup, that's right. We want a good fuck."

Even though Tina asked for it, she went a beet red to the roots of her hair. What did I just say? She asked herself. I'm a whore.

"But we don't want to rape or force you. It must be consensual. You're a typical woman with normal desires," Ted held her hand reassuringly. "There's nothing to be embarrassed about."

Within the ten years that the were-tigers had mingled with humans, they learned that the female Homo Sapiens were emotional in nature. They had also developed some human emotions and behaviors such as, empathy and rational thinking.

Tonight, they wanted to mate with Tina but she still had some reservations and they were determined to respect that. As the fast tune by the band continued and dancers on the floor wiggled and shook their booties, their body temperatures simmered down below boiling point.

"Wanna dance some more?" Tom was swaying his hips in front of Tina; his decreasing erection was still evident underneath his pants.

"No, thanks," she replied, her breathing had started to normalize.

When she was certain the fire in her body subsided, she felt a rough hand caressing the insides of her thighs. She stood up, startled. "Jess," Tom eyed her with pleading eyes. Her mind said no, but her body was rebellious, wanting to be fondled.

Tom pulled her back to her seat. "Let's play for a while," he nuzzled her nose.

Tina's panty was wet; her pussy was churning tissue juices as her arousal intensified anew. Under the tables, Tom had inserted his fingers under her panties and was stroking her clit. She squirmed in her seat as Tom flicked her clit with his index finger, repeatedly.

Ted's fingers were busy under her blouse too, fondling her nipples. She was half-reclined on the long chair, shuddering as they fondled and caressed her. Oh God, she thought. I have to get up, or I'll climax right here. The waiters were discreetly looking to where they were. It could be embarrassing.

With a superhuman effort, she slipped out of their grasp and ran for the door. Before Tom and Ted were able to react, she was already on the street hailing a taxi.

What's wrong with me? Tina castigated herself on her way home. It was what I wanted all along, and yet, I have run away from it.

Tom and Ted had the same thoughts. She was positively responding to them but why did she run away?

When she arrived home, Tina went straight to the bathroom. She needed to extinguish the fire inside her body. She stayed under the warm shower for nearly an hour, but she found out that no amount of water could assuage her burning need. Frustrated and angry, she grabbed her rubber brush, applied some baby oil to its handle and tried to insert it in her pussy. But it was painful. She cried in the shower, frantically massaging her breasts and pussy not knowing how to appease the smoldering fire within her. She had never climaxed while playing with herself. That moment her vagina was eagerly waiting to be deflowered. She wanted to be fucked badly.

It was Sunday the next day and Tina stayed under her blanket, not wanting to leave the warmth of her bed. Her desires remained as glowing embers in her body, tough to put off. She was afraid that Tom and Ted would leave her once they'd learn that she was a virgin, and sexually inexperienced. Her low self-esteem had constantly marred her progress in life.

For Ted and Tom, they understood Tina's predicament. They already knew she was a virgin, through the pure scent emanating from her body, and they believed that she was still discovering her femininity. She was at a crossroads of whether she should surrender to them or not.

"Don't worry. We'll have to woo her," Ted patted Tom's back comfortingly, as their shape morphed back to their yellow and white stripes. They growled at each other, baring their sharp incisors and ran towards the forest.

Tina stared at her large image in the mirror. Her hard nipples were pinkish atop the pale white skin of her big, soft breasts. They dangled down halfway to her navel. She tentatively touched her nipples and twirled them between her fingers. How would it feel to have Tom's or Ted's rough hand fondle them? She wondered. She shook her head and continued to dress up ignoring the niggling feeling coming from her pussy.

She wanted to hide herself when Tom and Ted reported to work the next day. They surely concluded that she was a tease.

"Hi, Jess. How are you?" Ted cornered her while she was preparing the table napkins.

She looked up and saw Ted's happy countenance. "I'm good," she managed to reply; amazed that Ted was indifferent to all that had happened the previous night.

During the entire day, they were courteous and good-humored. But they were still trying to seduce her - in their own charming way. Tom blew her a kiss on her way to the counter, and Ted wiped a spec of dirt on her face, touching her lips with his fingers. The embers inside Tina had begun to glow again. She watched surreptitiously while the men stood guard at the door, catching glimpses of their rippling abs and concrete muscles that were like hydraulic pumps whenever they moved their bodies.

Tina visualized those bundles of bronzed muscles sweeping to the v- curve below their waists and it made her mad with lust. Their penises must be as spectacular as their bodies. Her pussy vibrated with longing.

By the time the last customer left the pub, Tina was exhausted. She wanted to stretch her body in a bath tub full of warm, scented water.

She was ready to go home when Tom and Ted approached her. "We can take you home," Tom volunteered.

"No, it's okay. I can manage." You can take me home with you, she said in her mind.

"You're near yet so far," Tom sighed, giving up on her.

Tina seeing his morose expression felt sorry for him, "Okay, you can walk me home. It's only a few blocks away."

Instantly their faces lit up with elation. "That's great! Let's get moving then," Tom led the way. At least, they were making progress, he consoled himself.

The orange hue of the sky at dawn was picture-perfect. Stars were still visible amidst the incoming brightness of the morning sun. Tina loved her tranquil walks from the pub to her home. Home was a rundown two-room apartment that had a small well-manicured garden and a comfortable patio.

Tom and Ted walked on each side of her, like they were her personal bodyguards. Her heart warmed up to them, the burning ember in her body starting to glow and increase in intensity.

Tom caught her hand and refused to let go. "Don't be too harsh on yourself, Jess. Everyone needs company," he reminded her, his large fingers imprisoning her fingers.

Tina stopped breaking free and just allowed Tom to hold her hand. As they held each other's hands, the heat started to spread to her body, cloaking her in a warm glow of security. It felt good to have someone protect her. She hoped that Tom and Ted would remain by her side forever.

"A penny for your thoughts?" Ted asked, concerned.

"I'm thankful that you're here with me," she replied, becoming teary-eyed. "Hey, no tears," Tom lifted her face and kissed her full on the lips.

Tina withdrew and tried to free herself from both of them, but Tom refused to let go of her hand.

"Why do you keep refusing to acknowledge your feelings?" he queried, his voice mirrored his confusion. "Be honest and accept the fact that you want us too. It's not a sin to want another person's company."

"It's not a sin to make love, Jess," Ted agreed. Tina remained silent.

"If you're afraid of anything, you can tell us."

"I don't understand myself, as well," Tina finally spoke her thoughts. "I'm afraid and eager at the same time."

"Hey, no pressure. Just allow things to happen naturally."

Tina tightened her grip on Tom's hand and they walked leisurely, talking about the funny moments at work. Their laughter echoed in the stillness of the night.

At Tina's doorstep, Tom was still holding her hand. He bent his head and gave Tina a kiss. It was like a lighter that ignited the embers inside her body. She clung to him sucking his tongue and lips. She clung to his broad chest, hungrily.

Tom responded with equal fervor, sucking her lips and hugging her until her bones were ready to break. Tina struggled to breath for a few seconds before Tom rained kisses on her face again.

"Let's . . . go . . . inside," Tina gasped in between breaths.

They rushed inside, almost stumbling by the door as Ted kept paced with them.

"No, no, not you," Tina said to Ted.

Ted stood by the door unsure whether to do as Tina told him. Tom motioned Ted to obey her. Ted closed the door behind them and listened as Tom and Tina created a din inside, as they rolled on the floor and collided into objects in the small confines of Tina's apartment.

Tom carried Tina to the bedroom and laid her on the bed, the veins in his sturdy arms crisscrossing his skin like live electrical wirings. Tina clung to his neck as their lips remained glued to each other, tasting each other arduously, their lips making slurping sounds as they sucked and nibbled one another.

Tom's fingers went under her undies, fondling the petals of her vagina, exploring the deepest sensitive areas until they trembled, and she was begging for mercy. "Oh, fuck me, Tom, please fuck me," Tina pleaded, her whole body ablaze with desire.

"Not yet, my dear," Tom hoarsely whispered to her ear. "I'm so big, I can hurt you. Let's prepare your juicy pussy first," he continued.

Tom undressed her, his fingers shaking as he released her big tits from their bondage. "Hmmmm, how soft and full they are," he said, massaging them firmly but gently. His other hand was fingering her already moist pussy.

"Oooooh, oooooh, yes, yes," Tina moaned, as his adept hands continued their persistent sweet assault on her body.

When he felt her body twitching, he went down on her, tasting her juice with his tongue, while his thumb flicked her clit continuously. Tina was loudly moaning, "Oooooooh, oooooooooh, yes, yes, right there, eat my pussy,' she spread her thighs wide and lifted her ass to meet Tom's ravenous tongue.

He was still in his jeans and the enormous bulge proved to be painful for him. But it was not time yet, he thought. Tina tried to undress him but he stopped her hand when he attempted to unzip him. "Not yet," he croaked.

He kissed her clit and nibbled it diligently as she arched her back and gave in to the tremendous sensations that overpowered her.

"Ooooh, Jesus, yes, yes, harder please," she cried once more.

"Please allow Ted to join us," Tom stopped and looked at her. "I'll invite him in," he said.

"Please don't stop, yes, yes, whatever you want to do," she uttered frantically, in total surrender.

Tom opened the door and Ted was there standing, waiting right behind the door. His cock was already tumescent.

"Please fuck me," Tina pleaded once more, her pussy shuddering for attention.

Ted went down on his knees and inserted one finger in her pussy and slid it in and out. Tina went wild, bucking wantonly. "Aaaah, yes, yes. PLEASE . . . FUCK . . . ME," she screamed, grabbing Ted's fingers and grinding it to her cunt. While Ted was busy, Tom got rid of his clothes. Tina's eyes seemed to pop out of her sockets and her heart pounded when Tom stood there in all his naked glory. His arms were layered with ribbons of muscles that extended to his biceps. She reached out to get hold of his massive arm, while Ted finger- fucked her. "You're so tight,' he stated, amazed, trying to add another finger as he slid his fingers over and over again, in and out, of her love hole.

Her love juices were dripping and she was about to climax when Ted stood up to release his enlarged dick into his hands. It was the same size as Tom's, about 9 inches long. He growled giving way to his animalistic behavior, as his rod bolted upright to respond to his massaging fingers.

Tina's legs were now up in the air, and spread wide apart as she urged Tom to continue what Ted started. She grabbed Tom and prompted him to mount her but Tom stood beside Ted, masturbating. The sight of two bronze gods pleasuring themselves was too much for Tina to take. She touched her pussy and clit and masturbated too, while ogling their immense cocks. I hope I can climax this time, she prayed.

Tom climaxed first, he howled and then knelt massaging his dick. He inserted two fingers into Tina's soaked pussy. She gave a loud cry and her body shuddered crazily, going right and left and then up and down. "Ooooooh God, fuck, fuck, fuck," she yelled, when the waterfalls of her orgasm washed over her whole body. So this is what women die for, she realized. She's willing to die for another taste of it too.

Ted came next, sputtering madly as his stream of creamy, sticky fluid squirted out from his throbbing cock.

The three of them - with Tina in the middle - remained in bed for the rest of the night. They did not bother to wash the sweat, semen and vaginal fluid from their gratified bodies. Tina held both Tom and Ted's flaccid cocks in her palms. She couldn't believe that they grew to such enormous proportions when erect. She felt Tom stir and his penis juddered and increased in size.

But she fell asleep before it grew to its full size yet again.

When she came to, they were gone and she was left with the vivid memory of her foray into her sexual fantasies. It seemed unreal but the burning ember inside her had diminished to an insignificant glow, and the overpowering odor of their coitus was hanging in the air. But she was still a virgin no doubt. When will they truly fuck her? Her pussy started becoming wet again. She had work to do though, so she squelched her longing and hurried to work.

Before the break of dawn, Ted and Tom changed forms to give way to their animal nature. They had to do it, if they wanted to remain sane. It was their destiny to roam the forest and be wild and free, and to take on human forms to socialize with their half-species.

Back at work, Tina was thrilled to be with Tom and Ted again. There was a lilt to her steps and her eyes sparkled, turning her into a more beautiful woman. They exchanged ardent kisses whenever they can, and during breaks, the three of them stayed together to 'play', fondling and stroking their bodies, exploring their erotic zones and basking in the wonderful sensations.

Every time Tom caught Tina in the pantry, he took the opportunity to let her cum using his mouth and fingers. She was becoming juicier, he was overjoyed. That means soon I'll be able to stick my hard dick into her narrow cunt.

The pub closed at 1:30 AM that day. They were all exhausted, and were too tired to do anything afterwards. Although, there were suggestions of another tryst at Tina's house, it was cancelled when Ted revealed that he had a splitting headache.

It turned out that he wanted to talk to Tom alone.

"What's bothering you?" Tom asked, annoyed that Ted had opted not to go to Tina's apartment.

"I feel uneasy not telling Tina the truth," Ted retorted. "Shouldn't we tell her first before impregnating her?"

"Do you think she'd agree? She'll be scared out of her wits and may even report us to the cops," Tom reasoned out.

"If we don't tell her and she'll learn the truth later on, she might want to kill our offspring instead of nurturing it," Ted aired his misgivings.

Tom paused for a considerable amount of time before saying, "Okay, I understand your point. Then assume the responsibility to tell her."

How would I tell her? Ted was in a quandary. He remembered a fact revealed in geometry that he once read in one of his wanderings. It read: 'The shortest distance between two points is a straight line.' He will have to reveal the truth to Tina in simple terms, no beating around the bush. Time was running out and he had to act tomorrow.

After work the next day, Ted was waiting for Tina. Tom had purposely filed a leave of absence not wanting to complicate things.

Ted's plans wasn't as easy as he envisioned it to be because as soon as they had stepped inside her apartment, she rushed to him and showered him with passionate kisses, not allowing him to speak.

She was horny all day long and Tom's absence and Ted's avoidance had turned her irrational with lust. She wanted to be fucked badly. She clawed at Ted's pants and fumbled awkwardly with his zip.

"Wait, wait…hmmmm," Ted held her hands and avoided her lips as she fell on top of him. "Wait, Jess… wait, you have to know something before we can proceed," he covered his mouth with his hands. But his cock was becoming rigid and angry.

Tina ignored him, "that can wait," she knelt and nibbled his erection through her pants. Ted growled and craned his neck. His eyes turned yellow.

"Tinaaaa . . . ," he growled.

He knew he would transform any moment. He had always been the unstable one, morphing to his animal form whenever he was extremely stressed out. And he was agitated. He realized his hands were slowly turning into claws. He had to scram before scaring her to death. This was not his plan of revealing the shocking truth to Tina. He forcibly pushed Tina and ran all the way to the edge of the forest.

His claws receded and he sat atop a mossy stone, thinking of what he should do next. He decided against calling her because he may not be able to say everything he wanted to reveal. His last resort was to write her a letter.

Tom was waiting for him in their rented room. "Everything okay?" Tom asked impatiently.

"No. I wasn't able to tell her because she was all over me," Ted replied. Tom was shaking his head.

"And I was out of control as well, wanting to fuck her," Ted admitted his own fault. The next best course of action is to write her a letter."

So, they wrote her.

Dear Jess,

This may come as a surprise to you but we had no other options but to write you a letter. There's something shocking that you must know about us.

However, before we tell you, please remember that we truly care for you and we hold you in high regard. That was why we have chosen you. You're the perfect woman for us.

We're shape shifters – weretigers- to be exact. We morph into tigers every now and then. We're the only ones left of our species and we want to propagate our species before we become extinct. We have chosen you to nurture our progeny.

We mean no harm to the human race because we're half-human, half-animal.

We enjoy living in the human world as we treasure our times in the wilds too.

Please accept our sincere wish so that our relationship could prosper to something more meaningful and noble.

We hope you'll keep the secret of our true nature to yourself. We trust you. We'll be waiting for your positive reply.

Sincerely yours, Tom and Ted

They sprinted back to Tina's apartment and nervously left the letter on her doorstep. They slept uneasily afterwards, unsure of their future. There were many 'what ifs.'

What if Jess reported them to the police?

What if Jess kept their secret but refused to mate with them? What if …

**

When Ted ran off from her apartment, Tina was confused. Had she been too forward? She had assumed that Ted would welcome her advances because that was what they have been waiting for – her willingness to have sex with them. Apparently, it was not the case. Ted got scared and ran away. Did he know something?

She tossed and turned in bed, unable to sleep, searching for the rationale of Ted's strange behavior. She drifted to sleep for a few minute and then woke up again to a noise from the doorway. Did Ted return? Her spirits lifted, but when she peered outside, no one was there.

It was when she was going to work that she saw Ted and Tom's letter sitting at her doorstep. She returned hastily inside and opened the letter with anxious hands. As she read the texts, disbelief was mirrored on her face. This can't be true, she pinched herself. Incredible and remarkable, she admitted.

She remained seated for an hour, staring blankly into space, thinking how life was so strange. She didn't feel scared or angry though. What she felt was inner peace and calmness. She wanted to see them pronto.

They were not there at the pub, however, and she regretted not asking them about their address and phone numbers. Records at the pub revealed the wrong information.

All day long, Tina waited for them to appear before her, but to no avail. Nighttime and dawn came but there was still no Tom or Ted. She began to worry. Did someone catch them unaware? Maybe they were fearful she reported them.

There was no alternative for Tina but to wait for them in her apartment. She trudged home wearily and waited by her window, anticipating a knock or a call, but nothing came.

A block away, Tom and Ted were observing her. Aside from her apparent sadness, they noticed nothing was amiss.

"She must have accepted the truth," Tom remarked.

"Are you sure she didn't report us?" Ted wanted to be careful.

"We trailed her all day long, and she never went to the police station. And no cops visited her."

"Then, let's verify it ourselves." They had missed her terribly.

Tina was half-asleep when the knock came. She woke up with a start and hastily peered through her keyhole. Her face lit up when she saw Tom and Ted standing there, smiling. Hurriedly, she unlocked the door and pulled them inside.

"What took you so long?" she exclaimed, breathless.

They were speechless, not knowing what to say. Her reaction was so unexpected. How come she readily accepted them? They wanted to ask her but she was already kissing and embracing them that the few days of missing her had come to the forefront. Their cocks were up in a jiffy, eagerly waiting to be fondled.

Tom kissed her hard and played with her tits, while Ted caressed her thighs and vagina. But Tina protested, pushing them both on the bed. "I'm in charge now. Let me be your mistress," she said, all her pretenses gone.

She slowly undressed Tom, easing his shirt over her broad shoulders and rippling biceps. Then she eased him off his pants, while massaging his semi- erect penis. In an instant, it had ballooned into an elephant's trunk, huge and wiggling, ready to spring into action with its hundreds of elastic muscles.

Tina purred, "Ooooh, such a monster," caressing Tom's rigid, thick cock.

Then she did the same to Ted, kissing his gleaming skin and massaging his manhood until he began moaning in delight.

She knelt and slobbered over Ted's 9-inch cock. She held it in her hand and caressed it like a pet, cooing lovingly as her fingers slid gently against its sensitive surface. Her tongue met the crown as it emerged from her massaging fingers. Ted reached out to knead Tina's tits in return, caressing them as though they were precious dough for a special type of bread.

Tom could not wait any longer. He positioned himself behind Tina,

holding his engorged dick in his hand. He raised Tina's buttocks, felt for her vagina, and without preamble, rammed his dick into it.

Tina cried in pain, "Aaaaah, that hurts."

Her hymen was still intact but her pussy was drenched with her love juices giving off a musky, earthly scent. Tom withdrew his dick and tongued her pussy. His colossal muscles contracted as he went down on all fours and sniffed her cunt. He licked its outer folds, up and down and then around using his tongue.

"Ooooooh, yes, yes, that feels sooo good. One more time please," she clamored for more. Tom repeated the action until she was about to climax.

Tina forgot about the pain, her pussy was hungry for Tom's cock. "Fuck me now, please," she commanded Tom.

Tom knelt, lifted her ass to enter her pussy and penetrated her once more. She was on all fours lapping Ted's dick like a starving dog. Tom lifted his right leg and forced his dick into her tight wet hole. Gradually his dick entered her pussy. She felt a brief tearing pain that disappeared when his thrusts became faster and deeper. Soon, Tom was like a bullet train, unstoppable and charging at top speed. He humped her continuously as he tried to bury all of the length of his cock into the folds of her tight and willing cunt. She felt her vaginal muscles grip his cock firmly, not wanting to let go. The incredible sensations caused by the friction of her sensitive tissues traversed her spine and triggered hundreds of pleasurable nerve endings that jerked her body upwards. "Fuck, this is heaven, ooooh, harder, yes, yes," she writhed and moaned in pleasure as her orgasm overcame her. In the throes of her orgasm, Tina had momentarily forgotten Ted.

Tom rammed his cock into Tina, encouraged by her cries of pleasure. His sweat-drenched body and chiseled muscles, strained to achieve his own climax. He was desperate to cum. He kept thrusting, relishing the suction-like action of Tina's virgin pussy. When he withdrew his cock to thrust back in again, a squelching sound came out. This aroused him more, making him go nuclear, He roared and the wooden beams of the house shook.

Tina trembled anew with her incoming orgasm as Tom went on pounding her ruthlessly until she screamed again andclimaxed, wracking her whole body. "God, oh God, aaaaah, aaaah, aaaaaaah."

Her vaginal fluid erupted flowing with the blood that came from her ruptured hymen. This mixture soaked their groins as Tom hurled a horrendous growl and dug his dick deeper into her cunt.

Ted went on massaging Tina's breasts and kissing her, while caressing his own manhood. Now and then, he would fondle Tom's nipples and caress his back as he fucked Tina. When herorgasm exploded, Ted took Tom from behind, giving in to his animalistic nature. He parted Tom's buttocks and stabbed his anus with his throbbing dick.

Tom was used to Ted's anal fucks. They had fucked each other when they were not able to find sexual partners. Still, his anus was as tight as Tina's cunt, and Ted closed his eyes basking in the pleasure of a tight fuck. His precum provided the gel for his easier entry into Tom's anus. While he pounded Tom, he was also pounding him into Tina's pussy.

"Arrrrrrrrrrrrrrrrrrrgh, sweet Jeeezusss," Tom's eyes were beady and sweat mushroomed from his gleaming skin; his muscles were taut and distended, ready to exert tremendous power.

Tom growled and his claws started to appear, he growled once more as Ted rammed him from behind, intensifying the sensation. They went on for several minutes – Ted fucking Tom and Tom fucking Tina, their roars and groans of ecstasy pervaded the room. The bed creaked dangerously and the room quaked as they humped each other – nonstop.

Then Tina screamed like she was being tortured, "Aaaaaaaah, oh God, ooooooh, fuck me, fuck me. OOOOOOOOOOOH!" This time her orgasm was galactic, she thrashed and cavorted madly, her body seemed possessed as she twitched uncontrollably for several minutes.

Tom's ejaculation followed and he groaned out loud claiming his prey. Soon, the three of them were chorusing frenziedly as their bodies remained joined to one another, savoring the sweetness of their mating.

It was after 30 minutes that Tina stood up to clean herself up. She felt sore in between her legs and in her ass, but her body felt rejuvenated. The glowing ember of lust inside her was completely quenched for the moment. She knew it will start to glow once more, but for the first time in her life, she felt she was whole – a complete woman.

Tom and Ted had fallen asleep uncaringabout the overpowering stench of their after coitus juices. While they were sleeping, Tina prepared a sumptuous meal for them: Fried pork chops, sautéed lamb barley soup and braised rabbit with mushroom sauce. She was pleased with herself as she set the table for them.

As expected, they were famished after all the energy they had spent having sex. Tom and Ted had sniffed the delectable scent of food and their noses led them to the cramped kitchen.

"Jess, how did you know to serve us these kinds of dishes?" Tom asked. "Sit down were-tiger, don't play with your food," she kidded him. "Before we eat, I have a special announcement," Tina declared.

Tom and Ted had various questions they wanted to ask her too. How come she wasn't scared of them? How come she readily accepted their true identities?

"Can we ask the questions first before your announcement?" Ted interjected.

"My statement can answer all your questions," she stated confidently. "Huh?"

"Listen to me first, then I'll answer all your questions later," "Okay," Tom and Ted finally agreed.

"I'm not what you think I am," Tina said, almost in a whisper. They eyed her, unable to comprehend.

"I'm a weretiger too."

"WHAT?" Tom boomed, falling off from his chair. Ted was too stunned to react.

"Yes, you heard me. I'm one of you, a female of your species." They continued gawking at her in disbelief.

"Mother died when I was 12, and I was left alone to fend for myself." "But… we were told… uh…we're the only ones… left," Ted stammered.

"Well, it's untrue, because here I am. Aren't you happy about it?" Her face clouded. "You don't have to worry now about us becoming extinct."

Tom and Ted moved closer to Tina, their bulky and muscular bodies tensing, ready to pounce. But Tina held her ground.

She let out a menacing roar and her claws appeared gradually from her hands to her feet. She growled louder as her bones crunched and her body started sprouting hairs on her face, chest, abdomen and feet. With her final grumble, her head turned and Tom and Ted were staring at a Siberian tiger, its eyes menacing, its hind legs ready to spring and overpower them with its weight.

Tom and Ted jumped up and down with glee, "Let's transform," Tom directed Ted, and they morphed, as Tina, the tiger, stood watching them.

Before long, the three burly animals raced into the forest, their agile legs carrying them more than 50 miles per hour; their yellow and orange stripes glinted in the morning sun.

It was late afternoon when they came to rest near a cascading waterfall. It was one of the inmost parts of the forest. The silence was deafening. Only the sounds of animals and the murmur of the water can be heard. It was a perfect haven for rest and recreation.

The trio transformed to their human forms. Their claws retracted and their thick furs vanished into thin air and human nails and naked skin appeared. After a while, they had completely morphed into their human forms.

They were stark naked, and in paradise.

Tom was the first to recover. "You're one of us indeed, Jess. Welcome to the club."

Hey, guys, look," Ted was calling their attention, pointing at the crystal clear water of the natural pool below the waterfall.

They sprinted, naked, into the pool.

Tina stared transfixed at Tom and Ted. Although they were not horny, their dicks were still extraordinary as ever – BIIIGGG, she sensed her pussy quiver. It sent a rush of adrenaline into her head making her dizzy.

They were splashing water to each other on the pool, flexing their bundled muscles, while drops of water glinted tantalizingly from their golden tanned skin as their big, powerful arms became distended with their exertion. Tina watched, fascinated, the embers in her pussy began glowing again.

"Hey, Jess, what are you doing? Jump in," Ted cajoled her.

When she hesitated, Tom ran towards her and without a word, pinned her to the ground. Their naked bodies landed on the soft, verdant grass. His cock was already erect and its large veins were pulsating angrily. He slung Tina's legs on each of his shoulders and held her waist with both hands.

She was completely at his mercy and control. Then he pulled her towards his gigantic cock. His cock assaulted her pussy furiously – demandingly. In and out he fucked her, drawing her juices to lubricate his entry. He raised his head and howled as Tina's cunt tightly gripped his manhood.

"Keep fucking, damn . . . ," Tina was no longer in any pain. She was enjoying the superb sensations that only an excellent fuck provided.

Tina grew frantic, the fire within her was all-consuming again. With all her strength, she pushed Tom down and straddled him. She began riding him, sliding her torso against his groin as she went up and down, rotating her hips every now and then. Tom grasped both of her tits and squeezed them, feeling their warmth and softness.

With each of Tom's thrust, pin prick sensations scattered to her whole body, making her senseless with elation. It was as if the whole universe centered on her pussy and his cock that nothing else mattered. Tom held Tina's waist and then rammed her pussy into his dick continuously. She was begging for more, cursing, "Damn, dig in deeper, harder . . . ," she gasped.

From the pool, Ted was masturbating. His cock had grown hard as steel and it needed a pussy, as well. He hurried towards them, holding his cock in his hand. He stooped down and kissed Tina on the lips, sucking her tongue. He then kissed her neck and continued tracing the contours of her body down to her succulent breasts. He sucked her tits alternately, licking her nipples gently and twisting them in his tongue.

When Ted kissed her and fondled her tits, Tina's orgasm broke, "Holy shit, I'm cumming," she shrieked, slamming her pussy against Tom's dick as the volcanic eruption started.

Tom kept pounding, straining to reach his own climax as she rotated her hips to feel his mammoth dick shuddering inside her slick pussy. He climaxed and grinded his dick into Tina's cervix. "Rawwwwr . . . your cunt is so juicy. . . Oh God . . ."

Tom fell on top of Tina, exhausted, so Ted had to find fuckTina through her mouth. He dangled his hard cock above her face and grabbed both sides of her head. His 9-inch manhood entered her mouth and rested on her palate. She tasted his dick. It had a copper-like flavor and had a drop of semen at the tip of its crown.

Tina's orgasm was still ongoing but she raised her head to take Ted in her mouth. Her cunt was spasmodically shaking with the sweet sensations coming from Tom's deeply imbedded cock.

Tom finally rolled over, grunting with pleasure. He freed Tina's cunt, and Ted sprang up and hauled Tina upwards with him. He carried her, their groins attached, and leaned her against a tree trunk. He started bringing her down into his waiting enormous dick. As Tina went down, Ted kissed and sucked her breasts and sometimes her lips. His ripped muscles inflamed with his exertion. He was carrying the whole weight of Tina as her arms clung

to his neck. Their pubic bones produced slapping sounds as they fulfilled their organs' urgent need.

Tina whimpered in pain when her back hurt because of Ted's incessant pounding. Tom came to the rescue. He supported Tina by embracing her from her back. He tweaked Ted's nipples and caressed both of their bodies, while fingering Tina's anus.

"Mmmmmmmm, do it again, please," Tina urged Tom and Ted.

Tina moaned, her arousal was building up steam again. Tom's organ was up once more, eagerly wanting to enter an opening he had never entered before.

"Wait," Tom stopped Ted from thrusting. "I want to fuck you from behind," he expressed his desire.

Ted didn't disengage but held on to Tina, their dick and pussy tightly locked together. Tom had to help Ted lie supine on the grass with Tina on top of him. Tom then cuddled Tina's back and penetrated her anus. It was a scrumptious threesome position that they had never tried and their senses were on overdrive. When Tom and Ted initiated their pumping, Tina went mad, shaking her head from side to side and mumbling to herself. When their thrusts became steady and rhythmic, she screamed her heart out. Their cocks drove into her, relentlessly; the only remaining distance was the thin tissue between her pussy and her anus. Her anus was sore at first, but when Tom continued humping, the narrow slit widened and gladly accommodated his conquering dick. The incredible pleasure appeased her soreness and turned her insane with delight. When her orgasm came, it was humongous – a tornado that obliterated everything in its path. The delightful sensations went on, and on, and on until she was left copiously satiated and elated.

"Hmmmmmm . . . haaaaah . . . Oh Jesus . . . aaaaaaah . . . ," Tina's eyes were rotating wildly, and her body convulsed as the two cocks fucked the hell out of her.

"Fuck, fuck, fuck," Tom joined in the din.

 "Damn, you're so slick Jess," Ted groaned, expelling his hot liquid.

Tom ejaculated simultaneously with Tina and Ted followed a few seconds after. It was a momentous unforgettable occasion for the three of them.

"From now on, this is where we'll set up camp," Tom stated. "We will build our home here and nurture our species. Let's live in harmony with both animals and humans for a better world."

Grinning happily, Ted and Tina nodded their heads and embraced him in a group hug.

Story 17

Chapter One

The adrenaline rush going through my veins had me feeling like I was flying by the seat of my pants. It was always this way when I found myself in the presence of something so overwhelming that it felt like I was small in comparison. My breath was short coming in rapid gasps. The competition was what I lived for. There was no better feeling than fighting the velocity of Mother Nature at its best.

The finish line was right there in the distance and this was going to determine whether or not I was going to the world games in Vancouver or someone else would take my place. I knew I had all the tools to be one of the greats. It was as natural as breathing.

I straightened myself out becoming like a bullet down the slopes at a speed that didn't seem possible. Laughing was the only way that I could justify my actions. It just came out. I flew past the competition. I was behind from the beginning because I just couldn't get out of my own head.

I had to stop thinking about him and what I had found when I came home a little earlier than expected a few months ago. It wasn't that he was cheating on me. It was who he was cheating with.

Lisa was never very choosy when it came to those that spent the night in her bed. We were supposed to be friends and this was the reason why I wanted to beat her on the slopes. It felt good to see the disappointment in her eyes when I was the one that came over the finish line first.

"I didn't think you were going to make it and suddenly you were taking a few unnecessary risks. I've never known you to be reckless and that could have ended badly with many broken bones." My coach and mentor gave me the confidence to give the sport a chance. I was always good, but I became even better underneath her tutelage.

"I just knew that I had it in me and I was willing to do whatever it took. To succeed there has to be risks for great reward. I'm not going to apologize for an outstanding performance. I think we both know the endorsements have been waiting for the right one to come along. They need to see something special and I was willing to throw them a bone." There was no way that my parents could afford to send me to the world games in Vancouver. I was depending on these endorsements to give me a free ride.

"I want to talk to you about that and there's no better time than the present. I have some good news and some bad news. The good news is that the endorsements will be there when you arrive in Vancouver. The bad news is that we won't be getting our hands on the money until a few weeks after your performance. I've made some phone calls on your behalf and hopefully, someone will find it in their hearts to support you in this endeavor. I would pay your way, but my gambling debts piled up pretty quickly." I was the one that finally got her to admit she had a problem.

"I wasn't expecting you to pay my way and I'm sure something will come up at the last second. I've always believed in fate and destiny and I'm not going to stop now. Too many things have happened in my life not to believe there's a reason for everything." I was never a believer in the mumbo jumbo of psychics.

I did have personal experience with healing crystals and those things considered alternative medicine.

"I can't tell you how proud I am of your accomplishments. You're not the typical blonde ski bunny. You're flaming red hair is a signature we are going to profit from. I look forward to seeing your performance in Vancouver. If you can reach down deep like you did today then I see great things in your future." I remembered something in passing about family friends leaving the state of Colorado for a Canadian citizenship in Vancouver.

"I have an idea which should give me free lodging in Vancouver for the duration of my stay." I was only 5'3, 120 pounds of solid muscle where it mattered. In my youth, I was a little out of control and never hesitated to do something extremely careless. I lived for the pumping of my adrenaline and the racing of my heart at a million miles an hour.

"I'm still holding out hope there might be a sponsor that hasn't

already been taken. They usually fill up pretty quickly months before the event. I warned you ahead of time, but you said that the universe would provide. I never could quite understand your mentality, but I have to say that you always seem to come through in the crunch." Coach Adams was what I considered someone to emulate. I wanted her to know all of her hard work wasn't for nothing.

"I've sacrificed a lot to be here including my family. They understand this is my dream and they have given me their blessings to do whatever it takes to make it big." I had been secretly taking classes on the Internet to give me that safety net. I did believe everything had a purpose, but I was not foolish to think that accidents couldn't happen.

"I know all about your work ethic and how you have given everything to be here. I heard about your boy problems and I was worried that you were going to allow him to get the best of you. Emotions won't help you and there's no point in dwelling on something that is over. I've learned the hard way over the years to separate personal from business. It would be a good idea if you could take on the same trait. Don't let anything stand in your way and be your own destiny." She was a mother figure and I only saw my family on special occasions and holidays.

I was still getting over the sting of a relationship that should have been my support system. Unfortunately, I couldn't trust anyone with my heart after finding him in bed with another. Walking away wasn't easy and the key to my heart was shattered. I was still reeling from the effects and the vivid imagery of him on top of her of all people.

They claimed it was a mistake and they were only finding closure for the relationship. I knew they were lying and I decided to cut my losses before getting in too deep. Love was a fickle mistress.

"I'm a little more hardened and seasoned for my 22 years." My sex life was dismal and I wasn't about to find an available piece of ass to enjoy the pleasures of the flesh.

It was a distraction, but I did feel the burning desire to be with someone after the competition. Mostly, I would take matters into my own hands with some adult novelties I had bought for my collection.

"Don't underestimate the power of losing a man and what it can do to your psyche. This is a relatively fresh wound and my suggestion is that you find something to take your mind off of it. I've always found the best way to do that is by getting under another." The red and white ski outfit with matching gloves and boots molded to my body like a second skin.

"I'm not immune to a man's charms or the way they look at me with only one thing on their mind. I'm what you would consider a camel when it comes to satisfying those urges. There are times it becomes too hard to resist. It's been a few months and maybe that's the reason why he turned to another." I was finding excuses when I knew the only answer was that we were not right for one another.

"Don't do that and he's not worth the effort. Concentrate on the days ahead and not the past. Forget about it and move on. Giving him any kind of power only makes you vulnerable and weak. You can't afford to lose a step. The only stumbling block is whether or not you will have a place to stay when you get there." I knew that my father was in touch with those family friends I had been thinking about. I couldn't even remember their names. I got the feeling that maybe it started with a K or a C.

"I'll let you know how everything works out and by all means contact me if you hear of any other openings concerning sponsorship. I'm not holding my breath. I don't want to put anybody out even if it is my future we're talking about. I never want to be a burden." My passion for the sport was never in question.

My dedication was above reproach and it gave me a giddy little thrill to put Lisa in her place. The downtrodden expression on her face was a good way to exact a little bit of revenge for sleeping with my boyfriend.

Chapter Two

The chill in the air made those unprepared shiver in place, but I wasn't one of them. Others would want to live in paradise with the white sands and tropical drinks in hand. I was more at home with the snow swirling around on the roads. Each snowflake was different in their way. No one was identical.

I'd spoken to Kenneth and Carla with the phone number provided by my father. He never promised me anything and told me that it was in my hands. I couldn't imagine a better conversation than with the two of them.

They were quite tickled pink that I was coming to visit. They were thrilled to offer me free room and meals for as long as I was going to stay.

"You don't look anything like you did when you were 13." It was a statement that would have most likely come from a male, but this one was of the female persuasion. "I came to visit to look after your mother when she was sick. You were a rebellious child and you were lucky that you weren't my daughter. I've always been a big believer in punishing for misbehaving." I turned and found her hovering over me like an Amazonian princess.

She had big bones and her breasts were mountains onto themselves. There was no time during my youthful indiscretion that I had ever thought about being with a woman.

The skintight white sweater did nothing to hide her attributes. The high beams were easily her best feature not including legs that went to heaven and beyond.

"Carla, I was a bit bitter back when my parents were separated. I learned from my mistakes and I took my attitude into the arena of skiing. It releases endorphins, unlike anything I've ever experienced before." She got this smirk on her face and I began to think that I would have loved to have the ability to read her mind.

"You're too young to have the kind experience to render that kind of statement. I'm sure there's something I can come up with to give your body the same jolt of excitement you get from strapping on a pair of skis." I wasn't sure, but I could see that her nipples were quite noticeable through that sweater. It was possible she wasn't wearing a bra and was allowing the elements to tickle her fancy.

"Don't pay attention to my wife and she always gets this way when I don't give it to her on a regular basis. She only has herself to blame.

Introducing me to a cleanse involving disgusting smoothies and working my body until I am almost ready to pass out doesn't leave me much for bedroom activities." They were very comfortable with their sexuality and made it sound natural to be speaking to me in these terms.

"It doesn't look like you would have too many problems performing." I couldn't believe I had a pair of grapefruits to say something like that.

"We're going to have to be careful with this one, Kenneth. She has a mouth on her and doesn't mind using it. I do believe this is a great way to reunite old friends. I know you probably have a lot of training to do. The site for the world games is no more than walking distance from our house. I suspect you're going to need some fuel for the fire. I like to dabble in the kitchen and I've been boning up on recipes for what a growing girl like you will need to crush the competition." Her long black hair made me want to touch it and run my fingers through her locks.

"My wife is an amazing cook and I've been very lucky to have a high metabolism to burn off the calories. I had a health scare a few months ago and now we are on this healthy regimen. I've never felt better, but there's truth in the saying no pain no gain." His shoulders were huge and could easily manhandle me into submission. His chest was making it hard to sit still for any length of time.

I walked ahead of them. I could hear them talking and laughing supposedly at my expense. I didn't want to be the butt of anybody's joke, but I had a feeling there was more going on here than idle chit-chat.

"I've taken the liberty of making the guest room and I hope it's to your liking. We do have to warn you that we can be pretty loud in the bedroom when things become too hot to handle. He may not be able to give it

to me every day, but he does more than make up for it when we do find time to be together." Kenneth was born to fuck and the way that he looked at me made me feel vulnerable and exposed.

He wasn't the only one. Carla was also giving me images in my head I had never even contemplated before.

I remembered what my father said and he told me to be careful with the two of them. They were carefree and lived a minimalist kind of lifestyle with only what they needed and not what they wanted. He claimed they had a hipster vibe.

"I just need a warm place to lie down and I can do my share of the cooking." Her hand on my shoulder was soon followed by his with my legs ready to collapse. I was breathing deeply trying to compose my thoughts without alerting them to the moisture in my panties.

"You haven't lived until you've had my husband's sausage. It's very juicy and he likes to make sure that my appetite is satisfied. I would be remiss if I didn't say that there's always room for pie." It didn't sound like she was talking about food. The flex of his organ inside his tight pants showed me that her attempt at not so subtle dirty talk had gotten a rise out of him.

"I'm sure a growing girl like you likes a fair amount of meat in her diet. I know athletes swear by pasta, but I don't see why you can't have a daily helping of protein." It was his turn to get in on the act. I could literally feel him burning a hole in my ski pants from behind.

I was in the back seat with Kenneth and it seemed Carla knew her way around like the back of her hand. She navigated through the traffic and was very close to hitting a pedestrian. My heart was literally in my mouth and then my fingernails were gripping Kenneth's very strong leg.

I could feel the mushroom shape of his knob pressing quite distinctly down the left side of his leg. Holding onto it became my lifeline as she made my life flash before my eyes. It felt like I was compelled to massage the length of his pipe.

"It looks like we have found ourselves someone of like mind. Your driving either scares them to death or excites every part of them. I'm pleased to report that Sienna is the latter mentality. This one is going to be a firecracker." His statement made me understand this was not their first time indulging in extracurricular activities with another.

"It's going to take us some time to get back to our house. I know all the shortcuts, but the influx of tourists during this time of year makes it difficult. The windows are tinted and it would really make the time go faster if you were to go down on Kenneth. Show him that not every woman is the same when they show their oral prowess. I'm sure that he would enjoy making the comparison. I don't think I need to warn you he's a bit more than a mouthful." She was giving me the green light to take that nice piece out of his pants to get a closer look.

"Don't look at me and she has always had the power in this relationship. I would say you have gotten her attention not to mention the attention of another part of my anatomy." Those black jeans were making his excitement quite evident.

"I don't think I've ever met a couple quite like the both of you. It's not a complaint and more a statement of fact. I'm not usually this willing to jump into the deep end without water wings. I'm virtually a stranger and maybe that's a good thing." My fingers began climbing the long and demanding object of my affection.

Carla was licking her lips and watching in the mirror with her eyes blazing with the fire of passion. She wasn't blinking the entire time that I was pulling down his zipper and finding his briefs could barely contain what he had to offer. It was huge and I very carefully reached into feel his flesh with my fingers.

"You weren't kidding when you said it's more than a mouthful. I'm not sure that I'm going to be able to get into my mouth." I was hesitant, but I wasn't going to allow his size to be intimidating.

"It takes practice, but I'm sure you're up to the task. Go ahead and you have no idea what this does for me. I get off on seeing the pleasure on his face. I love seeing somebody else make him cum. I can be the voyeur. I'll enjoy how your lips will send him over the edge. We don't stand on ceremony around here." It popped free from the prison of his briefs with the long vein down the back quite pronounced.

"I hope you're not expecting a hair trigger and she doesn't call me the marathon man for nothing." He was probably daring me to pull out all the stops.

It was already drooling down the sides and the thick cream coated the fingers which were wrapped around his girth. Using his sticky lubricant, I slid my fingers up and down making sure to concentrate on the head. I was no stranger to a man's pleasure.

"I can attest that what he says is true and you're certainly going to have your work cut out for you. I want you to take it as a challenge. It wouldn't hurt my feelings if you're able to make him into your sexual puppet." Taking his knob into my mouth was followed by a short burst which caught me off guard for a moment.

Stroking and sucking at the same time was a good way to hear him moan in defiance. He was doing his best to stay still and I appreciated his attempt to allow me to do the work. It was quite a thrill to explore every single inch including the full balls. I was able to capture them and I wanted more room to maneuver.

"It would be best to get these things down around your ankles." I heard a breathless exclamation and I turned to see that Carla was gripping the steering wheel tightly with both hands.

I figured by now that she would have her hand down her pants, but she was fighting that natural urge.

"I like the way you think, Sienna." He helped to get his pants and his underwear out of my way.

Less than an hour ago, I was getting off the plane and now I was in the back of this truck about to suck an older man's cock.

"I can honestly say I've never seen anything this big outside of the Internet. I have searched, but I was unable to find something of this magnitude. I guess good things come to those who wait." I inhaled the head, letting it stretch my jaws and it forced me to use the slippery surface of my tongue to allow him entry.

"I would say you are a natural and some can barely lick the head.

Take your time and I want you to be as comfortable as possible." The seatbelt was hampering my progress, but I was making do with the space I had been given. It had been months since being in this position and it was like riding a bicycle.

"I had no expectations when you called us out of the blue. There's always a feeling out period and then we make our move. It didn't take much to get you with my husband's cock in your mouth. I wonder what it would take to get his cock in your wet hole. Perhaps, if I were to promise that I would sit on your face at the same time would help you to make the decision." They were contagious and were quickly becoming a guilty pleasure.

Chapter Three

Sucking his cock was a pleasure and I purposely slowed down my technique to keep him from losing it. There was no point in denying him forever. I was enjoying the way that he was squirming and how Carla was giving me her undivided attention.

"I haven't seen somebody suck his cock with that kind of enthusiasm in quite some time. You really enjoy it and it's something that we have in common. Coming here might be the best thing that you've ever done in your life. I know we are very happy with the results." She was having a hard time speaking clearly, no doubt with her body crying out for some kind of satisfaction.

"I would not be the least bit put off if you were to enjoy the view in a more profound way." I hadn't been able to consume all of him, but I was getting closer with each effort. His endowment was disappearing and I was soon touching my lips to his stomach.

"It's not easy abstaining, but I'm sure that you will make it up to me when we get back to our place. Keep doing what you're doing and let's see if you can finish the job before we get there." I was getting more confident with long strides of my lips moving up and down. I was touching on every nerve ending I could find.

"I was ready 5 minutes ago. You're driving me crazy and you know the more time you waste the stronger my orgasm is going to be." This was one thing I was counting on and building him up to the big finish was my pleasure.

"Honey, you may not know this, but girls sometimes hunger for the seed boiling inside you. There are times I find it necessary to hold you back for as long as possible. I do admit to a certain fascination with the way your face contorts into a mask of euphoria. That feeling building up is better than any drug on the market today." It began to pump and I squeezed off the flow with the head looking like it was going to explode.

Slapping the head caused it to jerk and squirt a little bit all over his knob. It was quite thick and I couldn't help myself to taste it with the tip of my tongue. This only produced more of the same. I was now anxious to bring this to an end.

Grabbing onto his cock head with my lips, I stuck out my tongue and began to swirl it in a maddening fashion. He was grunting his response and pushing his pelvis off the chair getting the deepest suction he could get from my mouth. My hand wrapped around him and was working in tandem until I could sense the inevitable.

"Keep doing that…keep fucking doing that… YESSSSSSSS." His moan of desire was followed by the bursting of the dam between his legs.

I sealed my lips around the crown, still working my fingers up and down without stopping even during this momentous moment.

"Yeah…just like that…drain him of every drop and leave him powerless to resist." Carla was definitely a woman after my own heart. There was real power in getting down to the business of oral satisfaction.

Swallowing it was an effort and he just kept firing shots of jizz into my mouth. I forgot what it was like to be on the receiving end of such volume. It cascaded over my tongue leaving streaks along the surface to the back of my mouth.

"I hope for your sake that you're going to clean up the mess you made. Don't forget about what my wife said about punishing for misbehaving. I have a good leather belt and I know how to wield it." I looked at him and I smiled while still moving my tongue in a frantic pace to get it all.

"Kenneth, I don't think you're going to have to worry about her." He tasted like the best dessert I'd ever put into my mouth.

There was nothing left by the time I was finished. The lingering aftertaste only made me want to do it again. He would need time to replenish, but I had another that still required my brand of satisfaction.

I carried my luggage, pushing it through the fresh layer of powder on the ground until I was standing in the threshold of their cabin. It was two stories and the varnished wood inside was something to marvel at. I was counting my lucky stars for finding sponsorship with people willing to take me by the hand in and out of the bedroom.

There was hot breath on the back of my neck and then a pair of lips signaled something more than a passing fancy down below the equator. It was a feminine touch and she managed to weasel her way into the back of my pants. She managed to tickle my rosebud and then moved further down until she could feel how soaking wet I was.

"Those panties are going to have to come off." Her hands roamed freely over my breasts, pinching the nipples and then she was undoing the button on my pants followed by the zipper.

I was frozen in place unable to move. I knew Kenneth was probably watching this display.

"I've never done anything with…a woman." My confession did not break me free of her tongue licking the fabric of my panties.

"You'll find that my wife is a good teacher." He took my hands and pulled them behind me.

I heard the snap of the leather and I tried to move but I was at their mercy. I couldn't have done anything to stop them. It was a good excuse to let them do whatever they wanted.

My sweater went over my head and my bra was summarily released.

He was soon biting my neck and pulling my hair. His tongue insistently moved around my lobe and then he tugged at it with his teeth.

It was good thing there was a couch right in front of me. I swooned forward over the top of the couch while biting my bottom lip from the pleasure being induced.

"I love how you taste and I could stay down here for hours just enjoying the sounds coming out of your mouth." She was tracing her finger

and then penetrating the interior of my scalding essence. "You're fucking tight and I only wish that I could feel what my husband is going to feel. I'm going to have to live vicariously through him." She slapped the cheeks of my ass.

Every part of me was being stimulated, but my mouth was currently looking for something to satisfy a thirst I never thought was possible.

Kenneth was completely naked, showing off his muscles, but the flexing organ of his excitement was getting a necessary reprieve. I reached out and my hot tongue was enough to seal his fate. He wasn't going to remain out of commission for long.

"I give you permission to get him ready for this hot little body." There was a trail of clothing starting at the door which made its way over to the couch.

"You heard my wife and I don't think that you should take the invitation lightly." He was standing on the couch, feeding me the power of his loins. It only made me that much more anxious to feel him inside of me.

"I love the way you suck his cock with your eyes claiming to be bigger than your belly. The way he bulges in your throat and how your eyes well up with the effort only makes me finger bang your twat even harder than I was before." She knew what she was doing and had me groaning with hungry determination around his member.

My legs were shaking and my eyes were looking up at him with this big smile on his face. He was having the time his life fucking my face and holding onto my ears for support.

"The way you look at me with your eyes glazed over gives me fuel for the fire. We should curb our appetite until after dinner." I was stunned into breathless silence when he extracted himself from the warmth of my womanly caress. He released me from the belt.

"I'll go into the kitchen and make us something for dinner. I have a decadent dish that will stick to your ribs." They left me hanging there over the couch naked and dripping down the inside of my legs.

"Sienna, you'll find your room upstairs on the left and this will give you the opportunity to freshen up. My husband will be up shortly with something for you to wear for dinner." I was unsteady on my feet and had to hold onto the railing on my way up to the second landing.

Stopping at the top, I was able to look at the progression of their marriage starting from their wedding day. She seemed unable to look him in the eye at the altar. Later versions showed a different woman and something had to happen to bring them to this freedom to explore.

I had to take a quick shower to douse the flames which they had caused by rubbing me the right way. I could've easily taken on a football team. They had stopped things before they could go any further.

"Carla requests you wear this to dinner." I expected to find some tasteful dress with just a modicum of skin showing. What I got instead was nothing short of scandalous. It was see through. I felt like I was a different woman wearing it. I wanted to give him a show, but he had already turned to leave before I had gotten into the garment. It was silky against my skin, but I knew it was going to put a spotlight on me. I was suddenly nervous and about to go to dinner with hardly anything on.

Tomorrow was my first day of training in this new environment and my coach was going to be there to greet me in person. She could barely afford her own ticket and how she made out for lodging was anybody's guess. I lucked out on finding a kinky diversion from the tedious amount of time that I was going to take to the slopes.

My breath was short as I descended the stairs leading into the kitchen. The aroma of some kind of stew was hitting me like a ton of bricks. She was standing at the stove naked from the waist down and Kenneth was sitting at the table naked from the waist up.

"I hope you are hungry for more than just food." Her tone was seductive and I reached for a chair only to have Kenneth hold it with his foot to prevent me from sitting down.

Chapter Four

I stood there motionless trying to figure out what their game was. He informed me by tapping the table that my seat was going to be right in front of them. I jumped when she slapped my ass on the way around to the other side of the table.

I sat down on his plate and he grabbed for the material before giving a yank. It tore like paper down the middle stripping me of the pretense of being demure. There was nothing complicated with the way that they were looking at me.

She sat down beside her husband to feast her eyes on the wet slit down the middle.

"There's always room for an appetizer before the main course. I'm a woman of considerable appetite." I was liberated of my clothes and she peeled off her sweater to reveal nipple capped mountains.

My legs were dangling over the side of the very well put together table. It was made of solid Oak. She pulled me towards her and was sensuously moving her fingers underneath me. The flitting presence of her tongue along the lips was bringing my little friend out to play. It was quite enlarged and she was denying me the pleasure of her lips wrapped around it.

I was soon kicking my heels out against the chair she was sitting on. I was twisting my head from side to side and sending some of the cutlery and dishes to the floor. She was injecting new life in-between my legs. Her ravenous approach was met with enthusiasm on my part.

Kenneth was stroking his hard on with his excitement bubbling over the top. He was waiting his turn. I had no idea a woman's lips would feel so amazing. It was giving me something to think about concerning the possibility of adding the other half of the population to my sexual repertoire.

"Damn…you two girls are really going at it. I don't see any reason why you would need me around. Wait… I think that I have nine good reasons." He was priming his stiffness and there was no denying he was ready to break through whatever resistance he was going to find.

My legs were over her shoulders and she was scratching the inside of my thighs to insert some of her dominance. I was craving something more than her agile tongue. The feeling was clawing along my lower extremities. Her finger made contact with my G spot and she took the opportunity to touch her hot tongue to my clit.

I came with my arms and legs flying in all directions. There was a litany of dirty talk making it hard for him to stand there any longer than necessary.

"I want cock… I want hard experienced cock… I want it now." My body was desperate and he was more than willing to take his place at the fountain of youth.

"I'm going to be right behind him and you'll be able to see me over his shoulder. I'm going to fuck you with his cock and set the pace for what is obviously going to be a mind blowing experience." I used to like my love making sweet, but this overwhelming lust was hard to contain.

"I have to have her and why do you keep her out of my reach." I felt the head begin to push against the already soaking and sodden lips of my sex.

It didn't look like it was going to fit and it was her hips which forced him to push past the first obstacle.

"I know that you can't keep your hands to yourself and this is my way to keep you from finding something else on the side. Go ahead and enjoy it on my terms. Don't even think about moving unless I give you permission." She had her hands wrapped around his waist and was slowly guiding the length of his pipe to the lips. They were soon kissing the shaft.

"You've always taken good care of me, but maybe you should sit on her face. We can look at each other while she satisfies us from both ends." She quickly got on the table and straddled my face with her clean shaven cunt right there for the taking.

"Tempting me with her tongue is dirty pool." She lowered herself and I slipped her the tongue at the same time that he was drilling the enormity of his appendage into me.

I screamed, but my excitement was muffled by how she was suffocating me with her thighs firmly closed against my head.

The table began to move. This kind of craftsmanship was hard to come by. They must've had it custom made to take the brunt of whatever activities they were planning on using it for.

"I get no better pleasure than fucking this little hole and watching you so close to climax that it isn't funny. I would love for all of us to go off at the same time, but I don't think the first time needs to be a photo finish." His head was repeatedly hitting the overhead lamp. It didn't seem to slow down the fire in his loins.

"Yes…you are a breath of fresh air and there's no better testament to what you are doing than how I am going to scream my head off." Her cream was delicious and I could've used a spoon and sat there devouring all of her. I was using my fingers to scoop out what was dripping out of her.

I could barely concentrate on the way that he was fucking me with relentless strokes of encouragement. He was stimulating every time he pulled all the way out and then rammed like a battering ram back in.

"I hope you know this isn't the only time we are going to attack you like this. It's the one caveat of living here which I'm sure you're not going to put up any fuss about. We like young women to share together and it's very rare when we find one we agree on. It's even rarer when we find one that is up to the challenge of being with a couple." The muscles in his l egs were fatigued, but he was striving to push the envelope.

"I want you to shoot your load all over her pussy lips. Come on…I know the signs and you're just about ready to blow. Let's see what I can't do to get you there quicker." It would stand to reason that she would know what buttons to push.

They had been together long enough and I was curious to see how he was going to react to what she was going to do to him.

She showed him her nails and then grazed them lightly down his chest concentrating on the hardened buds of his nipples. This caused his body to react with jerks of appreciation.

His head was thrown back and he was moaning loud enough for me to hear him even with her thighs blocking out everything.

Darting my tongue in and out of her worked in my favor. The friction of him along those wet lips and the inner muscles squeezing his inches brought forth more than I bargained for. I was screaming and he was uncorking the bottle and letting the champagne of his white hot seed escape. He pulled out and it streamed all the way to my neck. I felt like a glazed donut.

We lay there on top of the table sticking to one another and I was the icing in the middle. They had their hands wrapped around me and then we were sitting at the table eating the stew. She was an amazing cook and I kept looking at her. She wasn't bashful and it made me feel good to know that I was in capable hands.

"We don't want to give you the wrong impression of us. What you see here is us being selective with those partners that we are willing to share with one another. Standing by one another over the years brought to light some secret kinks. We've been honest with one another and it helped to solidify our relationship." Carla was holding his hand and then she was sucking two of his fingers giving me ideas for the future.

"You don't have to explain the dynamics of your relationship and I'm just glad to be a part of it. I'll be happy to do the dishes and then join you in the bedroom upstairs after I'm done." They were making eyes at one another and I was going to find them in the throes of passion.

The next few days were draining on the slopes and I was depleted until I was able to see them waiting for me on my return. Training for the games was nothing compared to the acrobatics I performed on a daily basis with one or both of them.

The sex was good for my stamina and I managed to perform better than my expectations. After the games, I moved in with them and I took a position where I was teaching the next generation how to become the next big thing.

I still competed, but it was at the request of my endorsements. I was living the life I always wanted to and all it took was a change of venue. I had the best of both worlds.

Story 18

The world tilted crazily around Daphne and she almost fell. If she had, it would have been a disaster, because the road was right there. The cars zoomed by her, ruffling her dark hair and her clothes, to close that she could have reached out and touched them.

Ahead of her, the bike that had almost knocked her flying rode on, unaware or uncaring of what they'd almost done to her. She gasped and one foot slipped off of the curb, and it was only by throwing the rest of her body out of the road that she was able to keep herself from going flying into traffic.

That was the good side. The only good side. The rest of it was a disaster. She dropped her backpack and all of her schoolwork went everywhere, papers flying freely. Weeks and weeks of college work that she'd been struggling through to start with. On top of that, her entire body weight landed on that one ankle that was on the road. It twisted, and Daphne cried out in pain as she fell hard.

She fell onto the sidewalk, though, instead of among the cars. But her injured ankle throbbed and burned with the force of the landing, and she closed her eyes, fighting off tears, sitting in the remains of her homework. A small gasp of pain was all that she allowed out.

Thankfully, there were people everywhere, willing to help her up.

Gingerly, she put her weight on her own two feet, only to whimper softly as red hot pain rolled through her.

"It's swollen," a helpful middle aged woman said. "You're going to have to see the doctor."

Daphne winced at the thought. Her doctor was very competent, but she was an older woman with a manner that was not particularly gentle. Doctor Spears got the job done, but she wasn't particularly nice about it.

Actually, she was pretty much the definition of a crone, and Daphne always hated to go to see her, with her cold hands, horrible fetid breath, and sharp dark eyes.

When Daphne tried to walk, though, she winced and had to grab onto a streetlight just to keep herself from falling over. She liked to be able to take

care of herself, but what if she'd seriously hurt her ankle? Maybe even broken it?

Bowing reluctantly to the inevitable, she pulled out her phone and made the call. As she waited on hold, she hopelessly tried to collect up her papers. Maybe there wouldn't be an appointment available for awhile. She could hope, right?

"Actually, there was a cancellation this afternoon," the unbearably chirpy, cheerful receptionist said. "Doctor Spears has an intern with her today, though. Is that okay with you? He's watching the doctor with her patients."

Ugh. Could it get much worse? First a cyclist tries to murder her, then she hurts her ankle, and now she had to be a test subject for some brand new doctor? Wonderful.

"Yeah, of course," Daphne said. She supposed interns had to learn somewhere, though she cursed her luck that it had to be on one of the rare occasions that she went into the doctor's office.

Hanging up, Daphne sighed as she looked around at the remains of her hard work. She was going to have to start all over again, and she was already having a difficult time staying on top of her work.

She never should have let her parents talk her into pursuing a business major. Maybe if she'd gotten to study something that she actually liked, something that she had some aptitude for, she wouldn't have been so worried and distracted that she'd let a bike almost hit her.

Sighing, she hobbled to the bus stop which had been her destination to start with. Instead of heading back to her dorm room to hit the books and get ready for the final exams, which would make or break her GPA for her junior year of college, she had to go off to get poked at by some horrible old woman.

Wonderful.

* * *

It only got better from there.

By the time Daphne got to the office, her ankle was swollen up like a balloon, and it throbbed horribly with every step that she took. Not only that, but it had started to rain, a light, misty summer rain that nevertheless soaked her, plastering her dark curls to her head and her thin, snowy white shirt to her body.

God, she could see her bra right through the fabric. She couldn't help but notice that as she walked past a storefront and saw herself in the window. Not only that, but her nipples were hard and pebbled, pushing against the fabric of her shirt.

Maybe she shouldn't have worn a bra; she couldn't help but muse to herself. She looked like a total disaster, bedraggled and soaked.

And that was just getting to the office. After hurrying there as fast as she could, she was told to sit and wait. She got there exactly on time, even with her injury, but she had to wait half an hour more before the receptionist, a ridiculously adorable blonde girl with a wide smile, finally called her in.

"Daphne, follow me, please!" The girl was actually sort of insulting to Daphne in her very happiness, especially when Daphne was having such a terrible day. Pretty and perfectly pulled together, with the sort of bubbly personality that attracted people without even trying, the woman got on Daphne's nerves.

So she wasn't in the best mood as she sat in the exam room, perched on the edge of the paper covered table. She pushed her hair back from her face, and for the first time, she found herself grateful that she was going to meeting with an ugly old woman, not a hot guy. The way she looked right now, that would be a severe blow to her pride.

The door opened and Daphne took a deep breath, trying to settle herself, to ready herself for chilly, talon-like fingers on her injured ankle.

That breath was let out in something that was closer to a gasp, because it wasn't the ancient Dr Spears who stepped into the room.

No, it was someone who must have lost his way, because there was absolutely no way in hell that a doctor could be as ridiculously sexy as this man was. Tall, with broad shoulders and a slender waist, the guy had these intense, sparkling blue eyes and full, sexy lips.

There was a hint of mischief around him, somehow, though his face was solemn enough. Something about the way those incredible, gorgeous lips quirked up at the corners. Daphne didn't know what it was, but it utterly fascinated her.

He was wearing scrubs, which was the only reason that she knew that he was a doctor instead of, well, maybe a model or something. Only this man, he was far sexier than any model that Daphne had ever seen. There was nothing androgynous about him, nothing at all. He was masculine and huge and if Daphne stood, she knew that he would dwarf her. And she wasn't a tiny woman. Yes, she was slender, but she was tall, for a

woman. And her 5'8 was at least half a foot shorter than his muscular frame.

Damned if he didn't fill out those scrubs better than anyone she'd ever seen before. How was this fair? He was the hottest guy that she'd met in years, if ever, and she looked like a drowned rat!

"I hope you don't mind," he said, and his voice was every bit as arousing as the rest of him was, rough and deep and very, very manly, "But I'm taking over for Dr Spears today. She's running late."

"Okay," Daphne said, and she wanted to shake her head, bemused by how breathless her own voice sounded.

"I'm Doctor Steele. Call me Liam," the dreamboat said, and Daphne pushed her fingers into her mass of dark curls. They were drying now, but it wasn't much of an improvement, because it made the strands rebel and fly in crazy waves and curls over her shoulders and down her back.

Doctor Steele. Damn it. Even his name was sexy. How was this fair?

"I'm Daphne," she found herself blurting out. "Daphne York." Stupidly, she held out her hand to shake his, internally kicking herself for being such a tongue tied idiot.

Doubtless, someone who looked like Doctor Sexy was used to it, though. He certainly took it in stride. He shook her hand briefly, and she stared, amazed, as her fingers disappeared into his huge, strong grasp.

"I know," he said, not unkindly. "I read it in your file. What seems to be the problem, Daphne?"

She immediately fell in love with the way that he said her name. His pretty lips caressed the two syllables, made it sound exotic and maybe even a little bit sexy. Of course, he could read the phone book with that voice and sound smoldering hot, sexy as sin. It wasn't that Daphne hadn't noticed good looking guys before, but this man, he was something else entirely. A whole new level of gorgeousness.

"My ankle," she said, pushing her foot out for his inspection. Luckily, she'd been wearing a light pair of sandals that was easy to pull off.

"Looks sprained," he said, and he reached out and put his fingers gently on her. Dr Spears would have poked and prodded and hurt her, but not Liam. His touch was careful and gentle.

And it may or may not have sent little shivers of delight through her to have him touch her like that.

Daphne's friends were always telling her that she needed to get laid, but she'd never had time for that sort of thing. With her parents expecting her to follow them in business, and keeping a close hold on her purse strings unless she did as she was told, she had to buckle down and keep herself working all the time.

She was starting to realize just what she'd been missing, though. "Does the pain radiate up this far?" the sexy doctor said, and his

fingers trailed up Daphne's slender calves, moving over the curve and slipping up to his knee.

It felt like a caress. It wasn't, of course. He was just doing his job.

But the way he looked into her eyes, it was almost bold, wasn't it? Or was it just her imagination?

Either way, a surge of heat rose within her, centered in the very pit of her stomach, and she felt moisture starting to collect between her legs. Her clit hardened and throbbed, and just like that, she was ready to go.

"Uh … no." Daphne pulled herself together enough to answer the question. A slight smirk touched his lips and he trailed his fingers up further, up an inch or two past her knees. A little bit more, and he would be getting perilously close to the hem of her skirt.

"Are you sure? No pain up here?" Oh God. He was flirting with her. Or was she just desperate for that to be true, to the point where she would make it up? No, his fingers were definitely slipping up over her thigh, which quivered at the touch.

"I …" She could tell him to stop, she figured. If she gave him the sign, she was sure that he would back off. His movements were careful, like he was testing her. He waited, and she looked into his big blue eyes, felt the overwhelming urge to run her fingers through his short, dark hair, to trace over those cheekbones which were so high that they almost looked like they could cut glass.

No. She wanted this. She'd never wanted anything more, never felt this desire within her that made her insides seem to burn and melt.

Wherever this was going, she was willing.

"Maybe it does hurt," she said, her voice very soft, almost too much for even her to hear. "A little. Um …" she felt her cheeks flame with embarrassment, yes, but also arousal. "A little further up."

He drew in a quick breath, and then let it out slowly. He hadn't been expecting that, had he? But he nodded, and then, much to her surprise and dismay, he pulled away from her.

Not for long, however.

"I'm going to bandage up your foot. It looks like a sprain." He was an intern, right? Pretty new to his role? And yet, he seemed completely confident in his assessment. He had a hell of a bedside manner, no doubt about that.

"Okay," Daphne said, or rather, breathed. She was having a hard time getting much volume into her voice, because the majority of her attention was focused between her legs, to where her clit throbbed and her cunt clenched, aching to be filled.

He was a study in contradictions. Clearly, he wanted to take care of her, even if he'd been touching her in a way that wasn't really appropriate. He was gentle when he bound up her ankle, but firm. More and more, she found herself fascinated by him in a way that had nothing to do with the physical.

Not that there was anything wrong with the physical. No, there really wasn't. It was all that Daphne could do to keep herself from squirming as he touched her. When he was done, he rose to his feet, looming over Daphne as she perched on the examination table. He reached for her, and she inclined her body toward him, barely able to breathe.

Whatever he wanted was just fine with her. She'd never been this willing to do anything before in her life. So when he started tug her light shirt over her head, leaving her bare from the waist up, there was no question about whether she was going to let him or not. She just did.

"Your shirt was wet," he explained, that teeny, unbearably sexy little smirk on his lips again as he looked down at her. His eyes skimmed over the shape of her slender waist, her full breasts, and from his expression, he liked what he saw.

"So … warm me up," she murmured, far more daring than she would usually be. Why not? This was already far too crazy, not at all what she would normally do, and she might as well ride this out.

Especially if it meant getting to ride him, too …

His hands slid over her rib cage and up to cup her breasts. He held them, his hands firm and warm, his thumbs slipping thrillingly over her nipples and teasing them until they stood out straight and hard and proud.

This was surreal. This was a dream. It had to be. The best, weirdest dream ever.

Daphne let her head tilt back, let her eyes slip closed, as she moaned her pleasure. She had to be quiet. She knew that. Any odd sounds might have someone opening the door, and that was the last thing that she wanted. So when he pulled closer to her, when he lowered his head so that he could wrap his mouth around one of her nipples instead, she buried her face in his broad shoulder, letting it muffle her noises.

As his mouth was busy, his tongue swirling over the sensitive skin of her breasts, his hands were working on something else. They gripped her skirt and tugged it up so that it was around her waist, more of a belt than anything else. And she, utterly dazed with pleasure, confounded with it, let him do it.

Lightning seemed to sizzle through her body, centered on his fingers, which stroked over the skin of her inner thighs. His fingertips got closer and closer to the tiny white scrap of her panties, which were thoroughly soaked through.

Neither of them spoke. It was like they were both in a sort of a daze, unable to keep themselves from doing this thing. It was so forbidden, and the place itself shouldn't have been arousing at all.

Somehow, that only made her body throb more. She'd always done what she was told. She was done with that, if only just for this one crazy afternoon.

Glancing down at herself, she couldn't fight off a moan. She was stripped almost naked, her shirt off, her skirt pushed out of the way. As she watched, he pushed his fingers into her panties, his fingers just barely grazing over her slick, swollen folds as he tugged her underwear down, carefully over her injured ankle, leaving her so bare and vulnerable to him.

Her breathing came in quick little pants as she gazed at him. She let her eyes roam over his body, taking in every detail that she could see.

Those scrubs, again, they shouldn't have been sexy, but on him, well, somehow he could pull it off.

It didn't help that he had an obvious bulge pushing out the front of his pants. It looked to be impressive, too, though she found that she was more than willing to see for herself. The way things seemed to be going, she thought that she might get the chance.

For a moment, they just stared at each other, and then he was kneeling to the floor. Before she could really grasp his intent, he was between her legs, nudging them open so that she was even more exposed to him than before.

For a moment, she couldn't breathe. In that moment, he lowered his head and his full, pouty lips brushed over her swollen pussy. She cried out, only belatedly remembering to push her own hand into her mouth to keep herself from being far too loud.

No one had ever done this to her before. No one had ever tasted her like he was doing. His lips caressed her slippery labia, licking up her juices before his lips fastened on her clit.

Gasping, she reached down and she finally got to do what she'd wanted to do from almost the first moment that she'd met him. She locked her fingers in his dark hair and moaned as she rubbed against him, grinding her cunt against his talented mouth.

It wasn't enough, though. She felt so empty inside, like she needed, more than anything else, to be filled. She whimpered and squirmed, not sure how to ask for what she needed, but he gave it to her anyway.

Moving very deliberately, he slid a finger deep inside her needy cunt, rocking it slowly inside of her. She grasped around that digit deeply, trying to pull it deeper inside herself, already needing more.

She was getting so close, too, and it would be easy to just lay back and let him work his magic on her. That wasn't what she wanted, though. If she was going to go temporarily insane and let the hot stranger doctor have her body right on the examination table, she was going to go all the way with it.

Besides, she just felt like all she wanted in the world was to be connected to him in the most intimate way possible. Her whole body strained toward him, her blood molten as it ran through her veins, and she knew that she wouldn't be happy until she was filled up completely.

So she tugged him up, her hands cupping his handsome face, and then reached for the strings that held his scrubs up. With a deft movement, she untied them, and the loose pants started to fall, clinging perilously low on his hips.

It only took one more impatient movement for the scrubs to be knocked free completely, and the most gorgeous cock that Daphne had ever seen was released to rest against his flat stomach. It was the perfect size, she thought, to fit in her hand, thick enough to fill her completely, flushed and shimmering with pre-come.

She couldn't keep her hands to herself. She just couldn't. Daphne reached out and touched him, moaning at the heavy dick that filled her hand just as perfectly as she knew it would. The skin was smooth, but he was so rigid, it was like holding a steal bar covered in silk.

She wanted it. God, how she wanted it. Her entire focus was on this gorgeous man, on the things he was making her feel. Her whole body was shaking just a little bit, heat racing through her limbs, giving her energy unlike anything that she was used to.

It was addictive. The more she got of him, the more she craved, deep down in the very secret places of her body. She used her grip on his cock to tug him closer, and spread her legs, only just barely remembering to be careful of her bandaged ankle.

"Do it," she whispered. He was hesitating a little, as though determined to make sure that she really wanted it, and she didn't want there to be any doubt. She wanted him. With a deep, almost primal, craving that filled her entire being, she wanted him. Needed him. Maybe even more than she needed her next breath.

He didn't make her ask twice. Shifting forward, he gripped her hips in his strong, hot hands, tugging her so that her ass was right on the very edge of the examination table.

That put her at the perfect height, and when he moved forward, his erection leading the way, he was right at the level that she wanted him.

His thickness rubbed over her, slipping over her clit, and she let out a deep, urgent, heartfelt moan and rocked her hips up toward the stimulation.

He'd gotten her really close with his mouth, and she was more than ready for more.

He gave it to her. Just like she needed. She rested her hands on the round curve of his ass, feeling the muscles flexing under her fingertips as he took that last step toward her. Wrapping her good leg around his waist, she pulled him even closer, her tight, wet hole sopping wet and so very ready for what he obviously wanted to give her.

One thrust was all it took. Yes, she was tight. It had been a long time since she'd had anyone take her. She'd never had anyone who was anywhere close to as big as he was. But he slid inside her easily, and she was so ready to clench around him, to try to draw him deeper inside herself.

"Oh my God," she said, and only just managed to keep it a whisper instead of a scream of pleasure. She gripped onto his shoulders, feeling the cotton of his scrubs beneath her sensitive fingertips and thrilling at the contrast of that propriety versus the pleasure he was giving her with that huge cock.

He kissed her suddenly, thrusting his tongue into her mouth, and she was glad for it. It kept her quiet, because as he filled her completely, as he sent little tremors of pleasure zinging through her body, she could have been far too loud. She whimpered and clung and rocked up onto him.

It was so filthy, being fucked in a doctor's office. Right on the table, where God knew how many people had been examined, he thrust so deep inside of her that she felt almost like they were only one person, the two of them.

It was perfect. The pleasure, even the slight bit of pain from being stretched around someone so huge, it was all utterly flawless. They kissed over and over again as their hips ground together, and he pumped away at her frantically, his face desperate.

He wanted this, needed this, as much as she did. It was so ridiculous, how this had happened. How she'd just fallen into this situation, but it was exactly what she needed.

"Come for me," he whispered fiercely, and she could feel from how he pistoned away inside of her that he was close, too. That seemed absolutely perfect to her, too, on top of everything else, that they would come together when they did.

"Liam," she moaned, feeling greatly daring, maybe just a little bit bratty. Was she allowed to call a doctor by his first name? She figured that the answer was yes, at least if said doctor was busy fucking her through an examination table.

The whole time, each and every thrust, she'd been worked up toward her ultimate pleasure more and more. Suddenly, it spiraled completely out of control, and she once more would have screamed if she hadn't had her mouth seized in a rough kiss, if his tongue hadn't stolen her voice from her completely.

Instead, her hands clutched at his shoulders, clawing at them, and she let her cries be muffled by his lips and tongue. Right there in his arms, she went to pieces, convulsing around him again and again as pleasure wracked her entire body, stole her breath, even, she could swear, stopped her heart for a few dizzying seconds. At the same time, he gave a muffled little "Mmph!" into her mouth, and she whimpered as she felt the first of his come spurt inside her. He filled Daphne until she was dripping with it, and his last few spurts were lubricated by his fluids which seemed to coax another few spasms of pleasure out of her.

Both of them were breathless as they looked at each other, and then Daphne laughed softly. She couldn't help it. Nothing was all that funny; it was really a sound of pure, unadulterated joy.

She hadn't been looking for this at all, but she'd found it, and she couldn't be disappointed about that. This wasn't who she thought she was, but that was part of what made it so damn exciting.

He pulled away from her, and all that he had to do to look completely presentable again was pull his scrubs up. Then he looked completely calm, cool, and collected, not to mention competent. She was impressed.

Of course, she still felt utterly wanton, and suspected that she looked that way, too. Her hair must be a mess, her tits were exposed, the tips still pink from his mouth, and her skirt was hiked up.

While she started to compose herself, he smirked a little bit at her, as though he enjoyed watching her struggle to present herself normally again.

"If your ankle is still hurting next week," he said, and he actually shot her a little wink, "Then come back."

She nodded, and he added as his smirk widened, "Make sure that you come to see me."

With just those few words, he made it clear that he wanted to see her again. To her surprise, though she'd thought that this was going to be a one time sort of thing, she was more than willing to see him again.

What had happened, there had been more than a touch of destiny to it.

Like they were meant to meet, and meant to have sex. She was very interested, very intrigued, and very ready to see where all of this led.

*****

It was a grade two sprain, Daphne had been told, on one of her many visits back to the doctor's office. A fairly serious injury that had taken almost two months to heal. Two months of coming into the doctor's office, two months of seeing Liam at least once a week, since she'd be damned if she'd see any other doctor. Two months of the most intense, mind blowing sex that she had ever even dreamed of.

And, though she hated to admit it, she was getting more and more emotionally involved with Liam each time they met. It was a stupid idea, and she was completely certain that she was going to get her heart stepped on until it was little tiny pieces. Even with that being said, even though she knew deep down inside that it was a terrible idea, she didn't seem to be able to stop herself from falling for him.

They didn't have dates. They had appointments when she came in to get her ankle checked on. This relationship, if it could even be called that, was entirely based on the examination room, the same one that she'd been in the very first time.

Each and every time, they did the same things, the same incredible, sexy, intense, amazing things. And each time, Daphne went in telling herself that she was going to hold herself back, but she never really believed it.

He was addictive. She dreamed of him most of the time, and tried to think of reasons to go see him more often. She even wondered what he'd say if she asked him to go see a movie with her or something, something more like a real date.

Not that she would ever dare do that. Not when he was so handsome, and he had a real job, too. He had to be, what, in his early thirties? And she was twenty one, and didn't even close to have her life together.

All she could be was a dirty little secret for him. Maybe that was okay, because her whole body craved him, wanted him, needed him. She grew damp between her legs every time she so much as thought about him.

This visit, though, would be different. Her ankle was mostly healed. The swelling was gone, as was the bruising, and most of the pain. It would take some time, but she'd been assured that she would be fine.

Which might mean, she realized, that this was the last time that she was going to see him.

Maybe that was the thought that had her sick to her stomach. Which had her stomach clenching and threatening to empty itself all the time, especially when she first woke up in the morning and after she ate.

Was losing him enough to tie her stomach up in knots? It seemed that it was. Or maybe her body just thought that if she were sick, she'd be able to go see him more?

She sat in the waiting room, nervously clutching at her purse. She wasn't on crutches anymore, and she'd dressed in a deliberately in a much more feminine way than she usually would, especially when going to see the doctor. Her sundress was just long enough to be decent, and she knew that the dark red flattered her golden skin and dark eyes.

In the mirror, as she looked at herself, she actually thought that she looked sort of hot. The dress even flattered her breasts, made them look larger and more swollen, the nipples hard and prominent and thrusting against the fabric.

She didn't wear a bra. She hadn't, not for any of the appointments that they'd had together. What was the point? They only really had a few minutes to work with when they were together, and she didn't want to waste any of those precious, magical moments in struggling to get clothing off.

She had become all about the easy access. Skirts with no panties, such as she was wearing today. If this was their last meeting, it would be one to remember. Maybe, just maybe, by the end of this appointment, he'd be thinking about her even half as much as she thought about him.

A girl could hope, right?

Damn stupid to have a crush on a doctor. He couldn't be more out of her league, really. More than that, though, it felt like it wasn't just a typical crush. Was she really stupid enough to have feelings for this man?

It seemed like she was. Her heart felt like someone was squeezing it when she thought that she might never get to see him again. But it was something that she knew she was probably going to need to see.

The receptionist, who Daphne had finally learned was named Tammy, gave her the huge, happy smile that she'd apparently perfected with much practice.

It was a sign of how much she'd been in lately that she actually knew the name of the receptionist, and had even formed a sort of friendship with her.

"You can go in, Daphne," Tammy said, assuming that Daphne knew the way. Which, of course, she did.

With her stomach churning, her whole body filled with stormy clouds of anxiety, Daphne walked to the examination room. Her ankle didn't even twinge. She really was better, damn it.

He was waiting for her in the room, as he had been for the last few times. If she didn't know better, she could almost think that he wanted to see her. Though that was doubtless wishful thinking.

"You look different," he said, and his gaze was warm and intimate, skimming over her body. It lit a fire inside of her, one that she knew that his hands, his touch, would only stoke. It took so little for him to get her going.

Besides that, it thrilled her secretly and deeply that he had said those words, had looked at her like that, before the door was even closed. It was a small, stupid little thing, yes, but there it was.

"My ankle is better," she said, just getting that out of the way. His gaze skimmed down over her body, down her long legs, to scan said ankle, and she helpfully held it out for him to see.

"I can see that. I have something to tell you," Liam started, and Daphne took a deep, deep breath, trying to brace herself. He was going to tell her that this couldn't go on anymore, she suddenly knew it. And the thought made her head whirl, and not just figuratively.

She put her hand down onto the examination table, her whole body swaying just a little. Immediately, he was there, helping her sit down. His arms were strong and hard, his body hot against hers.

"Are you dizzy?" he asked, and she took a deep breath, fighting her swimming vision, and nodded. She had to admit, she felt better in his arms.

"Yes. And I've been nauseous," she said, which made him frown, speculation in those gorgeous, brilliant blue eyes of his.

"For how long?" he continued, in pure doctor mode now. She liked him like this, usually, it was sexy as sin, but she wasn't exactly in the mood to enjoy it. Though that didn't stop a little thrill of arousal from racing through her body. Damn him.

"A couple of weeks?" Daphne frowned, considering her answer, and then nodded. "But it's gotten pretty bad in the last week or so. Since I last saw you."

His face was very solemn, with none of his usual faintly mocking smirking. He got a small, clear, sealed container out and handed it to her.

"I'll need a urine sample," he said, and then directed her to the washroom. When she came back, he was no longer in the room, and she sat down once more, wondering just what was wrong with her.

Whatever it was, it was a big deal. She could tell by that serious look on his face. And when he came back in, he only looked more intense.

"You're pregnant, Daphne," he said quietly. Oh God.

All of a sudden, it all made sense. The pieces came together and she knew that he was right. She was pregnant. Her breasts had been fuller, swollen and sore, and now that she thought about it, it had been at least a month since she would have expected her period.

"Pregnant?" She took a deep breath, and looked at him, feeling utterly helpless. What was she going to do? She still had one more year of school, and that was just for her undergrad degree. Her parents wouldn't be happy with anything less than a Masters.

Meanwhile, he was watching her face, and she could swear that those eyes saw everything. Deep into her soul.

"It's mine, isn't it?" he asked, but it was like he didn't even really need to. Like he already knew the answer to that question. Dumbly, she nodded. It was literally impossible for it to be anyone else's.

He walked toward her, and she tracked him warily, having no idea what he was going to do. At least he wasn't walking right out of the room. That was something. She wasn't alone with this.

Gently, he cupped her cheek, and then leaned in to kiss her. It was a different sort of kiss from the ones that they'd had before. One that was far sweeter and gentler than usual. Caring, almost, she could dare to think.

"What do you want to do?" he asked her, and without him needing to say it, she was filled with the utter certainty that he would support her, no matter what her decision was. That helped. It made the whole situation slightly less terrifying.

"I want it," she realized, her hand floating down to cup her tummy. It was still flat, but soon enough, it would round with a child. Their child. "I want this baby."

"What about school?" he probed a little bit more, and she realized that she was now talking to her lover, the father of her unborn child, and not the doctor any more.

"I never," she said, realizing the truth of every word as she spoke it,

"Wanted to go to school. I never wanted to be a business major." She paused, stunned by the words that she had never really allowed herself to think, or to fully feel. "I don't know how I'm going to do it, but I want to keep this baby."

"You'll do it with my help," he said, and brushed his lips lightly against hers.

Even that small contact was enough to make quivers of delight spread through all of her, all the way to her fingertips and even down into her toes. "If you want it."

She looked at him, and then a huge grin spread over her face as something that she hadn't even known was tight inside of her chest and stomach suddenly relaxed. Relief consumed her, and she threw her arms around his shoulders and pulled him close to kiss her again.

"Do you want this?" she whispered fervently. She knew that they were supposed to be talking, but his closeness was intoxicating, and she couldn't help but rub against him just a little. "Do you really want this, or is this just because you feel sorry for me?"

Before she bound herself to him, she needed to know if he just wanted to do it out of obligation. She wasn't sure that her pride would allow her to accept that.

"I want it. I love you," he said suddenly, and she gasped. She had never expected to hear those three words from him, even though she'd come pretty close to thinking them herself. "I want you. I want this family."

She kissed him again, this time much more passionately, and he returned it, plunging his tongue into her mouth and swirling it over herself. Her knees went weak and she was suddenly glad that she was sitting. Otherwise, she might have fallen.

Damned if the man wasn't a hell of a kisser.

"I want it too," she whispered, and she moaned, more than willing, as he hoisted up her skirt and bared her completely. She hadn't bothered with underwear at all today, and she was deeply pleased with herself for that.

She didn't want to wait any longer to have him inside her. Relief, it seemed, was a powerful aphrodisiac, or maybe it was just knowing that she had a future with this man that really got her juices flowing.

It wasn't just her, either. The front of his scrub pants was bulging out, stretched tight over what she already knew was an impressive erection. He shifted closer and she could feel it rubbing against her most sensitive areas, which made her moan and rub more firmly against him.

"I love you too," she admitted. It was crazy. They'd only known each other for a couple of months. The thing was, though, she knew it was right. Maybe it was utterly insane, but that didn't stop it from being what she wanted.

Reaching down, she freed his cock, her hand an expert on the motion after so many times practicing it. Without hesitation, she pulled him out, stroking him a few times as she tugged him even closer to her.

His hands ghosted over her flesh, his fingers pressing lightly on her firm, taut belly. She was still flat there, but she knew that he was thinking ahead to when she'd be rounded sweetly with the child that they'd both created.

It was heated, yes, and very passionate, but it was more than that, too.

There was something there underneath the sexual arousal, something that had more to do with love than lust. There was a world of difference between the two, she was learning.

"Lie down on the table," he directed, and she smiled at him as she did as he asked. Just like that, in a split second, he was on top of her, the little table luckily sturdy enough to hold both of their weights. "I want to look at you while I have you this time. I want to see your eyes while you come."

Hearing him say those words, that was almost enough to set her off right then and there. He entered her slowly, his hands grazing over her sides and down to her hips, and she wrapped her legs around him and canted her hips up to try to get him deeper inside of her.

As they moved together, as he thrust deep and slow inside of her, she felt tears come to her eyes. How was this so perfect? How was she actually in love with this amazing man, who loved her back? How was it that they were starting a family together?

It wasn't conventional, but it was right. The way he moved inside her, yes, but also the commitment that they'd made it each other. It was right, and it was perfect, for them.

"Liam," she said, savoring the sound of his name on her lips. "Liam, love, I'm so close …"

Miraculously, he nodded. Sweat shone on his forehead, making it glisten, as he pushed his cock deep inside of her, stretching her open in the best way possible, making her entirely his.

"Daphne," he gasped, and if she'd liked the way his name sounded on her lips, she absolutely adored the way hers sounded almost whimpered out like that. "Daphne, now!"

Just like that, she came, the waves of sensation rocketing through her and making her lose herself entirely in him just for a few seconds. She closed her eyes and held on tightly to him, refusing to let go as pleasure wracked her slender body and made her lose everything else.

At the same time, he convulsed and she felt the slickness of his hot fluids inside of her, coating her and filling her and making a silent promise that, if she was his, that he was hers, too.

"What did you want to say before?" Daphne belatedly remembered, as he rested his head briefly on her shoulder as though gathering his strength. This had been just as crazy intense for him as it had been for her, she figured.

"Hmm? Oh." He laughed softly, swiping his lips over hers briefly before standing back up. Being fucked on an exam table was sexy as hell, but it wasn't all that comfortable after. "I just wanted to say that Doctor Spears is retiring. I'm taking over her practice."

She started to laugh. She couldn't help it. It was a laugh of relief, yes, because even if she hadn't been pregnant, she would have been able to keep

seeing him. But it was also just sort of hilarious, really, because it wasn't like he could keep being her doctor.

He joined her, and helped her up off of the exam table. She knew, right then and there, without any words needing to be spoken, that she had just seen him for the last time. As his patient, at least.

As for what they would build together, well, that was the exciting part.

It would be them, him, her, and their baby, and they could build a family together that was just perfect for them.

Story 19

Chapter 1

It feels too good to stop.

My hand is wrapped around my cock, pumping in synchrony as the woman on —Busty Cougars‖ rides the man beneath her. He is young, like me, with that innocent wide look in his eyes while she looks fucking hot, staring down at him with fire only a woman who knows what she is doing has. God, I dream about having a woman like that worshiping my cock, riding her tight pussy up and down my shaft as her nails dig into the skin of my chest.

—Damn it,‖ I say through clenched teeth and shove a pillow over my face to stifle a moan. Last thing I want is for my parents to hear me.

Crap. Now, I can't see the porn. I throw the pillow off me and push my fist into my mouth so I can lay my eyes back on the sensual woman on the screen, rocking back and forth.

Back and forth. Back and forth.

The man's cock is wet from her juices and I imagine that it's my cock that's soaked from her wet, tight pussy. I'm pleasuring her. I'm making her cry out and moan, bringing her to the best orgasm of her life.

And mine.

—Fuck, that's it.‖ I stroke myself faster when she picks up her pace. Her lips are puckered and a singular drop of sweat drips down between her breasts and my tongue flicks out over my lips, imagining that I'm licking it off. I bet it taste sweet like candy.

Her wide hips stutter, signaling she is about to cum.

I rub my thumb under the crown of my cock, tingling my spine with my impending release. —Oh, yeah,‖ my eyes roll to the back of my head when my shaft spasms. Just a few more pumps. Just a few more seconds.

I'm deep inside her as her muscles tighten around me, milking the cum right out of my tightened sack.

—So good. Your cock feels so good,‖ she moans, slowing down on the man's dick—that I'm pretending is me—and her hands run through her hair, trying to catch her breath as her orgasm quakes through her body.

The first stream of come leaves me, spurting all over my hand. I cry out at the same time the pounding starts on my door and through my orgasmic sensations, I turn my head to hear someone who sucks the endorphins away, leaving me in a frenzy of panic.

—Mom!‖ I shout, covering my exposed, leaking cock with my comforter and reach for the remote to turn the tv off. —Can I ever get some privacy in this house!?‖ I snap, embarrassed that I had to wipe up fast, sitting there with my shaft in hand… knowing that nosy wench is out there listening again. The woman who doesn't believe in sex before marriage. Just as I got done cleaning and clothing myself fully, the banging on the door happens again.

Whew. That was close... Almost got me.

—I know what you're doing again! I can hear it through the walls! Get. Out. Of. My. House.‖ She punctuates her words with clipped angry words.

—What? Mom—‖

—No, Dustin. I will not have that under my roof. It is a sin. Do you understand me? If you want to do that, it will not be here.‖

—Mom!‖ I shout, throwing my legs over the edge of the mattress, making sure to cover my crotch area until the woody dies down. —You can't be serious.‖ I yell out. I'm baffled. —You'reoverreacting. Every guy does this.‖

I haven't even had sex yet. I'm probably the only guy that graduated high school to never have sex.Suddenly the door flies open and she barges in.

She stomps forward and lifts her hand, back handing me across the face. —Not my son. Not my son! If you no longer want to be that, then pack your bags and leave. I expect you out of my house by tonight.‖

—Tonight!‖ I yell, forgetting about the comforter and when I stand, my foot gets caught in the material, tangling in a tight vice. Tripping, I fall to my knees, barely keeping the hold on the blanket as I try to catch my breath.

—Mom, just calm down and we can talk about this—‖

—There will be no talking.‖ She bends down and grabs my chin with her fingers. Her lips are curled in a disgusting snarl, like she has never seen something grotesque in her life. —I will not have this filth in my home. You are the filth and in order to keep this home sin free and clean, you will leave.‖

Instead of getting upset, I nod, keeping my gaze locked on hers. If she wants to disown me for this, that's on her. I'm not going to feel bad for what comes natural to me. —Fine. I'll pack my bags.‖ I make sure to keep my voice steady and start thinking about where I'm going to go. I have money saved up. I've worked for the last three years, every weekend and summer. I've saved up enough to get my own place. Being on my own doesn't scare me.

—You are no longer a son of mine.‖ She lets go of my chin with a push and turns around, slamming the door behind her. The walls shake and the vibrations travel up my knees.

This moment was doomed to happen. My mother and I have been drifting apart since I was sixteen and to be honest, I started to feel like I didn't belong here. I'm older now, but it doesn't matter. She's still a bitch. Getting up, I toss the comforter away and fix up my black gym shorts and take a duffle bag from underneath the bed to start packing.

I'll leave the —Busty Cougars‖ disc in the DVD player as a parting gift.

Chapter 2

The morning sun pierces through the windshield, searing my eyelids and forcing me to wake up. I wince, lifting my arm to block the blinding rays. I give my eyes time to adjust and see that I'm parked at the local gas station parking lot. It's abandoned and hasn't been used in the last couple years.

Leaves decorate the pavement and the gas pumps have plastic bags over them, telling anyone that they are out of gas.

Since I'm here, I'm assuming what happened yesterday with my mom was not a dream and I actually got kicked out and got caught jacking off to porn.

—Fucking great, I mumble, rubbing the sleep out of my eyes. I have no idea where to start looking for a place. Opening the truck door, I step out and stretch, getting the kinks out of my tight muscles. I take a water bottle out of the back and grab my toothbrush and get the rancid taste of sleep off my tongue.

As I brush, I start brainstorming. I know there is an apartment complex off Grant Street, but I hear the woman that runs the place is strict. The town is small though and there are only two complexes to choose from. If either of those don't work out, I'll have to go to the town over.

I spit out the toothpaste and wash my mouth out, dab some water on my hands, run my fingers through my hair and take a look at my reflection in the window. I don't look too bad, a bit tired, but what teenager isn't?

—You can do this. Just explain your situation and everything will be fine, I tell myself as I hop back in my truck. I clench the steering wheel with my palms before starting the engine and pulling out on the highway. While I'm driving and come to a stop at a traffic light, I think about the fight with my mom and do my best to understand where she is coming from, but I can't. If I ever have a child, I will never turn my back on them like my mother did me.

She should have talked to me, helped me understand my urges, but instead, she gave up on me. And if she wants to give up on me, then I'm giving up on her. I let out a breath and relax when I come to that realization. Now that I'm not living under my parents roof, I'm not a boy, I'm a man. My life is in my hands now.

Coming to the next light, I see the apartment building on the corner. It's nice. It has trimmed hedges and tall trees, flowers blooming and vines creeping up the side like they built the complex in an abandoned garden. I turn on my blinker and take a right down Grant Street, only to flip my left turning signal all to pull into the parking lot.

My palms sweat. I've never had to do this before. I've never had to ask for a place to live. It's the most adult thing I've done in my life. —You can do this, I repeat my new mantra because mom certainly isn't going to do it for me. I climb out of the truck and run my hands down the front of my flannel shirt. I double check my breath and run my hands through my black hair that could use a trim. The slight click of the heel of my cowboy boots hit the sidewalk as I close the distance between me and the front office sign.

The window is open, allowing the breeze to roll in and that's when I notice her. She's sitting at her desk, twirling the thick of her long red hair in her hand until she circles it into a bun on top of her head. The smooth curve of her neck shows, and the flawless pale skin has my mouth watering. She fans herself and there are beads of sweat dripping down her neck.

Her eyes are shut, relishing in how good it feels to feel something other than hot, sticky air. I swallow the lump in my throat as I watch her through the weeping willow branches swinging in front of the window, giving me teasing glances of her. I can't seem to move my feet forward. I'm entranced.

Captivated. Bewitched. Enthralled.

Never in my life have I seen such a beautiful woman.

Taking a large calming breath, I gather my nerves and start walking again, pushing the main door open to the complex. The bell jingles above my head, alerting her that I'm here, and the air inside is thicker than it is outside, making it difficult to catch my breath.

The walls seem to have a fresh coat of paint by the fumes lingering. Grey hardwood floors are shining beneath me and I feel a bit guilty for not wiping my dirty boots at the door. It seems they have put a lot of work into this place.

Click, click, click.

Her heels kiss the floors as she comes from her office and down the hall. I can't see her yet, but the echoing of her stilettos gets closer.

And closer.

My heart beats faster, harder, matching the rhythm of the sound of her shoes. I need to act cool. I need to look appealing and sexy, like an older man would. I lean against the wall and cross my arms, keeping my back straight and chest pushed forward, staring at the door she's about to walk through to greet me.

The silver handle of the door turns downward, and the lock is freed from trim. Through the narrow window panel, I see a glimpse of her bright red hair. Her long, milky leg steps out when the door hits the wall with a soft thud. Her heels are black with a red heel. My eyes travel up her leg to a short black skirt.

I gulp, trailing my eyes over the tight fitted yellow tank top she has tucked in, suctioning tight to her large tits. Her cleavage is pushed up, almost spilling over the thin material and my eyes finally make it her face.

Her ruby red lips that are holding the end of pen and my immediate thought is that could be my cock.

Fuck, I'm starting to get hard.

She bats those long lashes at me that frame her green eyes, and I have to adjust my stance to hid my erection. This woman is older. I can tell by looking at her face. It isn't as plump with you but refined with experience and graceful aging. She can't be more than forty.

And damn it, she is everything my wet dreams are made of.

Chapter 3

—Can I help you?‖ her voice as a soft rasp as she steps forward, never taking the pen from her lips. She holds a handout to greet me and I'm stunned silent.

Like an idiot.

I still try and speak, but nothing is coming out of my mouth as I stare at her. I clear my throat when my face starts to heat and sweat starts to fall in my eyes. Damn, it got hot in here.

—Oh my, aren't you adorable,‖ she says. —I'm Victoria, the manager of Grant Apartments. What brings you in to see me?‖ Her eyes rake my body and her tongue flicks out over the edge of the pen, teasing the silver tip with the wet pink appendage. My eyes never leave her mouth. Too many scenarios are running through my head. I can't concentrate. How can I when she looks like that? She's dangerous.

I finally get my hand to work and meet hers, holding back a moan when I feel how soft her skin is. —I'm Dustin,‖ my voice cracks like I'm going through puberty again. I'm so fucking nervous. I clear my through and cough. —Sorry, do you have any furnished apartments available? I'm just starting out.‖

—Dustin. You're a cutie. Anyone ever tell you that before?‖

Great. Cute is not the word I am looking for. My mother used to call me cute.

—Not really,‖ I say, taking my baseball cap off and scratch the back of my head. It's a nervous habit.

—Well, isn't that too bad,‖ she clicks her tongue, raking her eyes down my body again. I can't tell if she is checking me out or not. —So, why here? Don't you have school or something? And follow me, I'll take you on a tour.‖ Victoria turns on her spiked heel and sashays away from me, swinging those wide hips that I want to reach out and hold.

Is she prying for information?

—Um, mom kicked me out,‖ I say, taking a right down the hall when Victoria does. I'm so embarrassed to admit that to a woman like this. She's accomplished, successful, and beautiful and I'm just me.

She stops at another door and slides a key inside, —Oh? What did you do? That's naughty. I don't know if I could ever do that to my children.‖

I trip over my feet from her statement and slam my shoulder against the wall.

—Are you okay?‖ she places a hand on my shoulder and her painted red nails dig into my shoulder a bit.

—Yes, sorry. I don't think I heard you correctly. You have children? More than one? Not possible. You are way too hot to be a mom,‖ the words slip out of my mouth before I can stop them.

She giggles and runs her fingers down my arm, grazing my skin with her sharp nails. Goosebumps break out over my body and I try not to tremble.

—Aw, you are sweet. You know how to make a woman feel good about herself, don't you?‖

—Just speaking the truth, Victoria.

—It's always good to be honest,‖ she stops in front of another door and that's when I realize we have been walking down the hallway for a few minutes.

—Now, this is a studio apartment. Furnished. Five hundred a month with utilities. It's large and has a view of the garden outside. It won't last long,‖ she pushes the key in, and I think it may all be in my head, but her ass pushes against me, rubbing slightly against my cock before she opens the door and vanishes inside.

—Wow,‖ I say, staring at her thick ass. Of course she has had kids. Only a woman with a real body like this has had them.

—It's a great space, isn't it?

I rip my eyes off the bubbly globes and take a look around the room. I didn't really care what it looked like. I knew I'd take it, one because I needed to, and two because it meant I'd be in the same building as Victoria. —It's nice.‖

—Here you have your restroom,‖ she flicks on the light and I peek my head around the trim, my face close to her shoulder as we look at the basic toilet, shower, and bathtub. I close my eyes and inhale, smelling her sweet perfume.

She smells like cotton candy.

I love cotton candy.

—It smells good,‖ my words come out more as a moan. —I meant your perfume, not the bathroom.‖

—Oh,‖ her hand lays against her neck as if she is shy, but I know that isn't the case. Victoria sucks her bottom lip in her mouth and glares at me with those emerald eyes again. —Want to take it?

—Take what?‖

—The apartment,‖ she pats my chest and lets it linger before grazing her body on mine as she walks away.

—I'd love to. I can pay you four months rent up front. I need to get a job, I know that might be a deal breaker, but I'm good for it.‖

—I bet you are. That's alright, Dustin. We will sign a month to month lease and then make it more permanent when you land a job.

—That's a relief. Thank you.

—You never answered my question, why did you get kicked out? Victoria sits on the bed and crossing her legs, rubbing my heel down her calve. She reaches behind and lets her hair down, shaking the red waves down her shoulders.

—Um, it's a bit embarrassing.‖ I scratch my head again. No way can I tell Victoria the truth.

—Aw come on, I'll tell you why I got kicked out, she rubs the spot next to her and I'm starting to wonder if…

No, impossible.

I shake the dream from my head and take a seat and dry my sweaty palms on my jeans.

—Tell me, I won't tell a soul.

—My mom heard me masturbating to porn one too many times, I guess, I groan, hiding my face in my hands. She chuckles and it makes me shake my head in complete shame. —I know, but my mom is religious and thinks touching yourself is a sin, so she kicked me out and said I was filthy.

—What porn were you watching? Victoria asks.

—What?

—Porn, which movie? her finger lands on my knee and starts to wander up, up, up, and right when she gets to my cock laying against my thigh, she slides back down.

—Um, well, I stutter, unable to focus as I watch her finger tease me. —It was, you know, I sound between a scoff and laugh escape me.

Her hand stops along the edge of my hard cock, not touching it, but just the warmth from her hand makes my breath come out in broken gasps. —Busty

Cougars,‖ I say quietly, watching the tip of her nail scratch over the hard outline of my crown. My eyes roll back and I try to breathe, I really do, but I've never had a woman touch me, and I never imagined a woman like this would ever touch me.

—Got a thing for cougars, Dustin?

She wraps her hand around my dick and squeezes. I nod eagerly and toss my head back, letting it rest on my shoulders.

—That's perfect. I have a thing for blonde hair, blue eyed men, Dustin. Men that are in shape,‖ she migrates her hand over my abs, —Hard in all the right places.‖ Her other hand cups my cock completely and my mouth falls open on a silent moan.

A bead of precum pools in my briefs and I swear I am already on the verge of coming in my pants like a…well, like a virgin.

—Are you already close, Dustin? she nibbles my ear before probing her tongue inside.

—N−n−no, I stutter.

—I bet you are. Are you a virgin, Dustin?

And this is when the woman of my dreams dashes out the door running.

Chapter 4

—You can tell me the truth,‖ she runs her tongue down my neck, blowing cold hair along the wet trail.

I nod, —Yeah, I am.

—That's so hot.

—What?

She tosses a leg over my lap and straddles me. Her skirt rises, showing a glimpse of her red panties. Victoria grabs my wrists and places my hands on the curve of her ass. It's soft and firm, the globes are thick, spilling over my palms. I squeeze, needing to reassure myself that this is happening and that it's real.

—You're so sexy,‖ she says. —All defined and…‖ Victoria grinds her pussy against my stiff erection, and I groan, nearly shooting cum into my briefs. She takes my bottom lip between her teeth, letting it go with a pop, —Hard. So hard, Dustin. Do you want me?

—So much, I admit on an exhaled breath as she kisses down my neck.

—That's good because I'm just getting started with you.

Victoria flattens her palms against my chest and pushes me back until my back is against the soft mattress and she slides down my body.

Don't cum. Don't cum. Don't cum. Not yet.

Nothing has happened yet! She hasn't even touched me, but the more Victoria grinds herself on me and her wet sheath soaks my jeans, the more inevitable my release becomes. I hold my breath, I count, I think of my mother catching me red−handed, but nothing is working, not when Victoria's hands are unbuttoning my jeans.

Glancing down, Victoria gives me a lustful stare with those green eyes behind those long lashes and it does me in. I grunt, shamefully while basking

in how good it feels to cum to something that's more than porn. A wet spot forms in my jeans and my back bows off the bed, hating that I shot off like that, but damn it, how can I not?

Victoria is everything I've ever wanted in a woman and she is getting me so worked up, I can't even control myself.

—Oh, now if that isn't the best compliment a woman can receive then I don't know what is, Victoria unzips my jeans and the slack from the zipper loosening my pants has me gasping when she dips her hand inside and pulls out my semi−hard, cum−covered cock. —Aren't you a big boy? she hums in appreciation, leaning down until I can feel the puffs of her breath over the sensitive tip of my cock.

I whimper. I actually fucking whimper when her hand wraps around the sticky shaft, covering her palm in my seed. Deciding I need to see more of this, I prop myself up on my elbows, waiting with hopes and dreams that she wraps those pretty lips around my cock.

Instead, she stands straight and takes a step back.

I begin to panic. I don't want this to be over yet. I need to redeem myself. I can be better than what she just saw. At least, the version of me in my mind can be. My cock is hard again, leaking cum from my last orgasm still. I'm about to ask her what's wrong when she lifts her skirt and takes off her panties. Inch by excuitiating inch, the red lace comes to view down her thighs.

It's nothing but a flimsy thong. The sexiest thing I've ever seen.

And she throws it at me until the wet part of the material that cupped her pussy hits my face and falls to my lap. I grab it, fisting it in my hand and bring it to my nose, inhaling her sweet scent.

—You are naughty, aren't you? We are going to have so much fun, Dustin.

My cheeks heat getting caught sniffing her underwear, but she seems to like it. Her nipples are hard, tenting through her bra and tank top. She turns

around, giving me the find curve of her backside and takes a step backwards to me. Gathering the red locks of her hair that flow down to her ass, she pulls it out of the way as she peers over the curve of her delicate shoulder. —Can you get that zipper for me? I can't seem to reach it.‖

I swallow when I reach out for the small black metal clasp. My hands are shaking and I'm having a silent conversation with myself that this isn't a big deal. People have sex every day, but for some reason, I can't help but feel like this is a legendary occasion for me. I pull down the zipper and slowly, her round ass cheeks show. When the zipper stops, I gain a little confidence and tug the skirt down over her hips until it falls on the floor in a useless pile.

Never in my life have I seen something so beautiful.

While she has her back turned, she yanks her top off, dropping it on the floor by uncurling her fingers from it. Victoria is only left in her bra and my eyes eat up every inch of her. She has two dimples decorating the curve of her lower back and I draw lazy circles around them with a finger.

—You are so beautiful, I admit, taking my other hand and skimming it down the divot her spine naturally creates down her back. The silk of her bra slides against my fingers and I decide while I'm here to unhook it. It's red as well, sexy, standing stark against her pale skin. Each strap on her shoulder falls, until the only thing keeping the bra up is the crooks of her arms since she has her hands against her breasts.

Victoria spins around to face me, her red silk bra barely covering the under curve of her tits. She has a dashing of freckles on her chest and my tongue twitches with the urge to trace and connect them. She flips her hair over her shoulder and closes the distance between us, dropping her hands for her bra to fall. Her perfectly rounded mounds are in my face, the rosy beads tempting me.

—You're a little overdressed, baby, she fists my flannel shirt in hand and rips it down the middle, tearing the buttons from my shirt. Tiny taps hit against the wall from the round plastic and her nails rake down my bare chest, leaving superficial red lines.

This is it. It's happening. Fuck, it's happening. God, please don't let me shoot off again.

She hooks her fingers over my jeans and briefs and yanks them off, only for them to get caught on my boots. Victoria kneels, not bothering to take off my boots and takes my cock in her hand again. I look big compared to her palm and the sight is making me feel more confident with every second that passes.

—I knew the minute I saw your puppy dog eyes, the innocence, I wanted it for myself, Dustin.‖ Victoria flicks her tongue out around the crown and my eyes close involuntarily from the pure ecstasy shooting down my shaft. —Is that okay with you?‖ cock in hand, she traces her plump lips with my angry, bulbous head and it causes my entire body to tremble and spasm.

—Take it. You can have it. Take it,‖ I say a little too eagerly.

—That's what I wanted to hear.‖

And then, quicker than a blink of an eye, she swallows me between her lips, taking me all the way to the back of her throat until the tip hits somewhere deep down. My hands fly to the back of her head, tangling with her red hair as she sucks me.

—Fuck yes,‖ I hiss, watching my cock sliding out of this sexy woman's mouth. —That feels so good.‖ I can't take my eyes off her. Every time she comes off my cock, leaving nothing but the tip in her mouth, she probs the slit with her tongue, gathering the precum that's dripping out of me. Her hand has a tight hold around me, jerking me in harmony.

She hums, moans, and closes her eyes, as if I'm the best fucking thing she's ever tasted. The familiar tingle starts at my spine again and there is no way I'm going to ruin this again. Not so soon. Without warning, I pick her up in my arms and throw her on the bed, her _fuck me' heels still on.

I admire her for a moment, memorizing how her red hair fans above her like a halo, brighter against the black comforter. Settling between her legs, I grab her ankles with my hands and explore, dragging my palms down the soft, hairless calves.

The closer I get to the apex of her thighs, the wider she spreads her legs, showing her pretty pink pussy with a path of fiery red hair above it. My mouth waters for it. Her folds are wet, glistening in the light, teasing me with how sweet she is. I just know she taste like honey. I know it.

I drag my lips down her thighs, doing what comes natural to me and considering it is my first time, I still want to make her feel good even though all I have to go off of is instinct and anything I picked up watching porn.

Victoria grabs her tits, kneading them for a moment before pinching her tightened nipples the closer I get to the most sensitive part of her body. My stomach is flat against the bed and face is just inches away from her pussy. I grip her hips and yank her closer until my nose gets tickled from her bush.

Her lips are waxed and smooth, putting her sheath on display even more.

Nerves freeze me as I stare at her and a lump forms in my throat that I swallow down, thick and audibly. It has to be good for her or this will go from the best experience, to the worst.

—It's okay, I'm going to teach you how to make a woman feel good Dustin. I'll tell you everything you need to know,‖ her voice is low, full of desire and want. A want for me.

That spurs me on and while her pussy is still beautifully intimidating, I close the distance between us and take my first lick of a woman. Her nectar bursts over my tongue and I immediately want more of the juice. I dive in harder and lick faster, spreading her sheath with my fingers so I can get dive in to get a better taste.

She moaning, tugging my hair with her hands and those spiked heels are

digging into my back, but I love it. I try and remember what I've seen, eating at her sheath until she explodes. I roll my tongue up, searching for something small that sets her off. At least, it does in porn.

—Up more,‖ she moans and arches her back. —There, there! Suck my clit into your mouth.‖ Her voice is broken,and her hands slam against the bed, gripping the comforter as she cries out from the bundle of nerves I'm sucking into her mouth.

I'm taking note.

—Slide two fingers inside me and curl them in a come-hither motion.

I do as the lady says, probing her tight entrance with my index finger and push inside. Her warmth, her tight channel, if it feels this good against my finger, I can't imagine how good it will feel once it's my cock. I rock my hips against the bed, needing friction to calm my throbbing shaft and slide another finger next to the other, and pump.

—Yes, she writhes and thrusts her hips in my face, grinding her pussy against my lips harder. —Harder. Fuck me with your fingers harder,‖ Victoria groans.

Again, I do what she says, quickening my pace until my forearm aches and the wet sounds of her pussy echoes in the room. I curl my fingers her and hit something spongy that gives a little and it drives her crazy.

Victoria bucks wildly, crying out and panting heavily the longer I do it. I keep her clit in my mouth and my fingers knuckle deep inside her, pumping and curling them like she says. —Oh, yes!‖ she screams, her back levitating off the bed. —Dustin,‖ she chants my name and my cock spasms and a stream of cum hits the bed sheet. I hold back the rest of my orgasm, not wanting to let go just yet. —Dustin, don't stop!

I never plan on stopping, ever. I want to stay like this forever.

—I'm going to cum. Dustin, you're so good, you're so good at this, more, more, more!‖ she yells, but I can't go any faster. My hand is getting tired, so I nibble on the sweet sensitive piece of candy in my mouth and that's all it takes for her.

Victoria's body stops moving. Her inner muscles clap down around my fingers. She stretches her arms above her head and a gush of cream lands on my tongue, sweeter than sugar. I hum in appreciation and relief.

So much fucking relief and pride.

I just made an experienced woman cum. Damn, if that doesn't make me feel good.

She grips me by the root of my hair and yanks my mouth of her pussy, interrupting all my thoughts. I get one last look at her pussy. It's swollen from my affection, wet from my spit and her cum.

—Come up here and let me get a taste of that mouth.

I crawl over her, licking up her flat stomach. I kiss each breast, giving a good suck on each nipple before I brace my arms on either side of her face. My cock settles between her legs and the thick muscle of my shaft is against her wet heat. I feel it. It's dripping onto my cock, teasing it, begging me to enter her.

She slams her mouth against mine, shoving her tongue between my lips. —I love how I taste on your tongue,‖ she says, making me want to lose control all over again.

Her lips are soft and warm, and she tries to take over the kiss, but I've had enough of that. I want to do this. I grab her jaw with my hand and steady her. She smiles, I feel it against my lips. Victoria wraps her arms around my neck and lets me discover the depths of her mouth.

We lazily kiss for what feels like hours, but the desperation gets to be too much, and soon the slow kisses turn frantic and desperate. Victoria reaches between us and takes my cock in hand, and I groan from the tight hold as she positions me against her entrance.

And then tightens her legs around my waist and flips us until I'm under her and she on top of me.

Oh, fuck yeah. This may be my favorite position. The view is un-fucking

-believable. I can see the underneath of her breast; how swollen it is from how big they are. Her waist is small, and her stomach is taunt. Underneath her belly button there are a few stretch marks, they tiny and faded. I only notice them because I am devouring every inch of her body, taking in every detail that I can.

I think the stretch marks are hot. It shows she is a normal woman that's lived a life full of memorable experiences. Dangling form her belly button is a green jewel that matches her eyes, making me want her more. It's simple and sexy, adding to her sensual nature.

Sitting up quickly, I lick along her chest, connecting the freckles I've been wanting to taste since I've seen them. She pushes me back down with more strength than I thought she had, gives me a wicked grin, and slams herself down on my pulsating shaft, her pussy swallowing me to the root.

Every muscle in my body tenses. I toss my head back and grit my teeth together when my sack pulls tight to my body and my shaft fills of my release, begging to let go. I shake my head and hold breath, curling my toes as I try and get through these next couple of seconds. That's all I have to do.

She claws her nails into my chest as she lets out a small whimper, —You're so big. You stretch me so much, Dustin. You feel good.

—You feel good too, I say through a shaky, broken breath. A tickle of sweat flows down my face as I hold back from coming inside her. My eyes round and I look back and forth around us as if a condom will magically appear next to us. —Condom?

She bends over and licks from my chin up to my top lip. —No need to worry. I can't have anymore kids. We are just having fun, no worries, no stress, for as long as you want. Victoria starts a slow rock back and forth.

My orgasm subsides a little from her words from the promise of feeling this more. Victoria uses my chest as leverage to gain support and speed. She leans down, pressing her breasts against my chest and takes my mouth in a messy kiss. I meet her thrusts, my sack slapping against her ass as she uses me.

I'm nothing more than a toy for her. I know that. And I have no problem giving her what she wants. She flips her long hair back and the ends are whips against my cheek, leaving a slight sting. I bring my hand up and slap her ass, getting a little carried away and shescreams, holding my hands against her meaty ass.

I help her rock faster and her brows furrow and her lips part. Those hips stutter and the sounds spilling from her mouths are pornographic. Victoria doesn't say a word, she doesn't have to, when she orgasms, I feel it. I feel the muscle squeeze me, her nectar drip down my shaft until my sack is soaked,

and her moans are long, consisting of mumbled words that stroke my ego.

—Yes, Dustin! Oh, yes. Your cock is so good. More, I want more,‖ she plays with her nipples as her orgasm courses through her.

She slows the pace down, tired from cumming and the last spasm of her muscles clenching around me has me shooting my seed into her, coating her channel with my warmth, filling her infertile womb. —Fuck, Victoria!‖ I shout her name and uncurl my toes now that the pressure is gone to preform well.

—Oh, hell, I toss my forearm over my eyes as I try and catch my breath. This is by far, the best moment in my life.

—Mmm.

I hiss when she touches the base of my cock, where we are still connected. I drop my arm to my side and watch as she brings her cum−drenched fingers to her mouth, sucking them clean.

My dick twitches in response when she gives me a knowing smile. —You taste good,‖ she reaches between us again, gathering more and brings the white cream to my lips. —Taste yourself.

Like I'd ever say no to her and deny more experiences. With a tentative approach, I flick out my tongue and gather my cum off her fingers.

Victoria smiles wide like I've really pleased her and bends down to give me a kiss. —This is just the beginning, baby.

And I'm already dreading the end.

Epilogue

I unscrew the cap on my water bottle and take a large gulp, then squirting some all over my face and bare chest. It's a hot summer day and these lawns aren't going to mow themselves. I'm on the lawn of the day–Victoria's.

And like every week she is outside, wearing a bikini that barely covers her nipples just to drive me crazy as the sun kisses her skin. We've been having sex since that time in the apartment complex, and my young heart as kind of fallen in love with her even though I know this will never go anywhere. She's given me everything I've ever dreamed about. Plus, how can someone not lose a part of their heart after having sex so many times with the same person for a year?

She'll always be my first...everything. Even if this is just for fun, I'll never forget her.

Walking over to her house, dragging the mower as I walk, and there she is. All miles of milky skin, glistening in the sun. I greet her as I always do, —Ms. Williams,‖ I pour water down my chest again and she slides her big black sunglasses down her nose to stare to check me out.

She bites her bottom lip and holds out the bottom of sunscreen to me, just like every other time. —Can you get my back, Dustin? I don't want to burn.‖

—Maybe you should go inside instead. I'd hate to see that skin turn pink,‖ I bend down and lick the shell of her ear. —Unless, it's from my hand spanking your ass.‖

Her hand cups my cock and squeezes, stealing the ability for my lungs to breath. —You better come make good on your word then. Victoria gets up and saunters away, peeking at me over her shoulder before she disappears inside.

I chuckle, adjusting my cock, and run inside to get all the experience with my favorite M.I.L.F.

SEXY WOMAN BANGED BY HUSBAND AND BLACK MAN

My husband knew that I had long wanted to have a sexual experience with a black guy and, as my thirty-seventh birthday was approaching, he decided to give me a night of sex like I wanted.

For some time I had been provoking a mulatto, Jeremy, who has an eyewear store in the area where I live, a beautiful, fine and distinguished man. I would look at the models with him and let him glimpse my tits, compliment him on the dress and the care he had in the store. I tried to go there less and less dressed and more and more willing to let him look at me, but he looked at everything and then in the end he never took the right step.

I was beginning to believe he was gay, because a real man can hardly resist temptation, and I am in a rather eloquent form.

But by now I was stubborn, I wanted to do him and this was becoming a fixed nail.

That evening I decided to go on the attack with Robin walking out the door with distracted, actually spying on me.

While he was opening a bulletin board to take some models by himself, I touched his beautiful hard ass, approaching me and showing him almost all my tits, which were hanging naked in a wide dress.

"Madam, you have the advantage of making clear and precise choices," he said to me without taking his eyes off my breast.

"You are one who knows about it and, if you want, we have the pleasure in the evening at home to serve a good coffee for friends".

"Of course I'll come for coffee and I'll bring you a nice model, which you'll surely like".

"All right, come by at 9 o'clock."

I squeezed his cock from above his pants and kissed him on one cheek telling him that he would find me perfumed.In the evening he came beautiful in a suit and tie and brought me, in addition to glasses, a bouquet of wild flowers with a card with "To tame a wild flower" written on it.

I was already unwinding just at the thought of what would happen, but I tried to stay with a certain decorum, being a good hostess. Robin went out for about half an hour saying that he would come back for the big party.

I enjoyed all the possible preliminaries with that fantastic macho guy.

I sat him down on the couch and stood over him showing my gratitude.

I only had a rather short dress under which I was not wearing anything and finally he started to touch my leg.

I kissed him wherever there were no clothes, I even threw lukewarm coffee on him to lick it through his hair, while his rod became a sword.I dripped like a whore, he understood and shared all the excitement of the situation, but he wanted to wait for the return of Robin to go to his room.

He began to masturbate me with fingers that looked like little cocks that were so long, tickling my clit and penetrating me with more fingers.

I had reached my first orgasm when the door opened.

As my husband arrived, he undressed me naked and invited both of them to follow me, I went into the bedroom. I immediately crawled on all fours and touched myself, by now eager as fuck, while they undressed. As soon as he was finished, Jeremy stood behind me and began to penetrate me without much preamble, but slowly, while I offered him to sheep pussy and ass. He took both holes alternately while I moaned like a bitch.

The more I squeezed the pussy, the more he would slam me; when the pussy was too wet, he would put it in my ass with a decisive blow making me scream with pain, but above all with pleasure. As he felt it flowing freely, he put it back in front of me where there were no obstacles to penetration, my moods enveloped him immediately, delaying his orgasm.

Robin was next to us and saw himself while inciting us and describing to Jeremy the dangling of my melons that he could not see.

Then he wanted me to take him up the candle in the ass in order to suck the nipples as long as nails. I let him in and took to shake me and let my moods run down his pubis. Jeremy screamed with pleasure and, after a while, I flooded my anus with hot cum while Robin cum on my tits.

I took myself off that pole and licked him greedy and he wanted to do the same to me. We shot ourselves a sixty-nine to shit and even Robin offered me his cock to clean.

Then he went to the kitchen and took a chocolate Bavarian cake and began to spread it on my body. They began to eat it licking it and contending for the parts above my erogenous zones.

I was a lake again and they two with hard cocks.

I made Jeremy lie down and I made me get inside, slipped without problems, then it was Robin's turn to put it in my ass with a few strokes.

I started screaming like crazy with those two magnificent cocks planted inside.

It seemed like it wasn't their first experience with a woman in the middle so they were good at fucking me.

Sometimes I could feel them both inside together, I felt like they were touching each other inside me. Others instead took turns to put it inside me, now Jeremy, now Robin while I no longer understood anything.

They began to change positions and my husband from underneath, while he was fucking me, he held my tits as if he wanted to burst.

They fucked me for a long time making me come several times, then they laid me down and cum on my face and tits together.

Before I could venture their cocks to clean them well, Robin opened a drawer of the bedside table and pulled out two big rubber fouls.

He gave one to Jeremy and together they kept banging me with them.

By now I could hardly stand it with their real cocks in my mouth and hands and the fake ones in my two holes. I could feel them burning, but I liked it anyway and didn't object to anything. Just as I had a little breath, I would take a cock in my mouth and suck it while I was beating the other one.

In the end, they got so horny that they were banging me in that way that they covered my face with semen again.

At this point I was really exhausted, I went to the bathroom to wash myself, even though I smeared a lot of their semen on my tits, which I like very much.

When I came back Jeremy had already dressed, I put on a robe to accompany him to the door and, before leaving him, I kissed him, inviting him back whenever possible.

He told me that only a madman would not come back and that next time he would bring a surprise.

I really deserved those glasses!

CPSIA information can be obtained
at www.ICGtesting.com
Printed in the USA
LVHW102021020621
689027LV00009BA/962